My Story

Sophie's Secret War

Jill Atkins

For Liam, Callum, Ewan and Isabel – hoping they'll
grow up into a peaceful world

While the events described and some of the characters in this
book may be based on actual historical events and real people,
Sophie Ridel is a fictional character, created by the author, and her
diary is a work of fiction.

Scholastic Children's Books
Euston House, 24 Eversholt Street,
London, NW1 1DB, UK
A division of Scholastic Ltd
London ~ New York ~ Toronto ~ Sydney ~ Auckland
Mexico City ~ New Delhi ~ Hong Kong

First published in the UK by Scholastic Ltd, 2009

Text copyright © Jill Atkins, 2009
Cover illustration © Richard Jones, 2009

ISBN 978 1407 10865 0

Printed in the UK by CPI Bookmarque, Croydon, CR0 4TD

2 4 6 8 10 9 7 5 3 1

The right of Jill Atkins to be identified as the author of
this work has been asserted by her in accordance with the
Copyright, Designs and Patents Act, 1988.

Normandy, France 1939

Sunday 25th June

Mama gave me this book last Christmas, and today is exactly six months since then so I think it's about time I wrote in it! First of all, I was going to use it to practise my English. I suspect that's why Mama bought it for me. I've been learning English for a couple of years and I love it. But then I changed my mind. I've decided to write a diary. I'll keep it secret. I don't want anybody reading my private thoughts – not even Yvette Bertrand. I really like Yvette. She's been my best friend all my life. We do everything together and share everything, but I'm not sharing this diary. I won't even tell her I'm writing it.

How shall I begin? My name is Sophie Ridel. I was thirteen on 25th February. I've got long, dark hair and I'm quite small for my age. Not like my brother, Sebastien. He's fifteen and he's tall and blond. We're always arguing, and Mama's always moaning that she's sick of hearing us. It's Sebastien's fault. He insists on annoying me.

We live in a little village in the middle of the countryside. Papa works at Mr Masson's farm, which is close by, just across the railway tracks. Our house is quite small. We've got

3

a kitchen and a living room downstairs and three bedrooms upstairs. You have to climb a ladder from the kitchen to get upstairs. My room is really tiny, but I like it. I'm lying on my bed now, writing this. It's so peaceful living here. I don't want it ever to change.

Monday 26th June

I hate Sebastien! He always has to be one up on me. Today, he challenged me to a race home from school. He didn't have his bicycle with him so I thought it would be easy, but as I pedalled round the last corner, there he stood, right in the middle of the road. I braked and skidded and landed in a patch of nettles. I yelled at him then I spat on the palm of my hand and patted my legs. The white lumps of the stinging nettles were already beginning to show. Olivier Masson was there, too. The pair of them stood towering above me, laughing. I was so mad, especially when I noticed a scratch in the red paint on my bicycle. Then I found out how Sebastien had managed to get home so quickly. He had a lift across the fields on Mr Masson's tractor. The cheat!

Tuesday 27th June

I feel a lot better today. When I had relaxed a bit yesterday, I went down the garden to the hen house. I let myself in and the hens clucked and fussed around me like they always do. I sat down on the end of the feeding trough, listening to their chattering and watching them scratching and pecking in the dirt.

I told them about Sebastien, about Mama moaning and about Papa always being busy out in the fields. As usual, the hens made sympathetic noises. They always understand. That's what I love about them. Some people say they're stupid creatures, but I know better.

After a while, I looked towards the house. Mama was swinging the level-crossing barriers across the road. That's her job. She has to open and close the gates every time a train goes through. Mr Masson had driven up on his tractor and was waiting on the other side of the tracks.

I heard the whining of the rails then the rumble of the engine as the train came round the bend. I closed my eyes. Soon I felt the earth trembling, and I was surrounded by a cloud of grey smoke. I love that smell of coal smoke and oil.

Then the train whistle squealed. It made me jump, even though I hear it every day. I opened my eyes and watched the trucks rattle by on their way to the sugar-beet factory on the other side of the village.

A few of the hens chattered nervously and one hid under the nesting boxes, but most of them ignored the train. They are used to it. Mama opened the gates and the tractor chugged across. I stood up and opened the nesting boxes. There were ten brown eggs. I carefully lifted them out and put them in my basket, thanked the hens and let myself out of the run, making sure I fastened the door. I don't want a fox to get in among my beautiful hens!

Wednesday 28th June

The news is always bad lately. It's all the fault of a man called Adolf Hitler. I don't know much about him except that he lives in Germany and everyone says he's doing some dreadful things. I don't like the sound of Adolf Hitler.

Thursday 29th June

When I got home from school today, I climbed up to my bedroom and did my English homework. After a while, Mama called up and asked me to take Grandma some eggs. I love going to Grandma's. Mama said she's a bit worried about her and told me to check up on her. I put three eggs in my cycle basket and pedalled off. Sebastien yelled at me and tried to make me fall off my bicycle, but I ignored him. I haven't forgiven him yet.

In five minutes, I had passed the church and was leaning my bicycle against Grandma's hedge. I ran inside and kissed her on both cheeks then put the eggs on the table and drank the home-made apple juice she gave me. I told her that Mama was worried about her. She laughed and said Mama fusses too much. She's probably right! Then she asked me what I've been doing lately. When I told her about my English she went on and on about it. She can't understand why I want to learn it. That's old people for you. She's always telling me she was ready to leave school when she was thirteen like me and how she was working up at the chateau by the time she was fourteen.

She asked me if I've got a boyfriend. Well, I really like Georges Dubois. He's so handsome and all the girls are in love with him, including me, but I wasn't going to tell her that. I felt myself go red and she noticed. She held up her hands and teased me about being in love!

Friday 30th June

Last day of school! We've got two months off. Yvette and I are going to do lots of things together and I'm going to keep away from Sebastien as much as possible. Maybe I'll get to see Georges Dubois a few times!

Saturday 1st July

All the adults seem to be talking about Adolf Hitler. I wonder why he's so important. He doesn't come from around here so why do they keep talking about him?

Monday 3rd July

Today, Yvette and I cycled to Veules les Roses. It's a village right on the coast with a steep white cliff at each end of the bay. It's only a few kilometres away so we go there a lot. We swam in the sea, messed about on the beach, laughed a lot, sunbathed and helped the fishermen when they arrived on the incoming tide. Then we climbed up the cliff path and lay on our fronts on the edge of the cliff. We looked down at the rocks and pebbles below and watched the waves as they came in and out, listening to the crash and the hiss as the water sifted through the stones. I feel peaceful when I hear the sounds of the sea. I've always loved it.

Later on we went to see Aunty Régine. She's Mama's sister. She lives with Uncle Thierry and their little boy, Charles. Uncle Thierry wasn't there. He was at work. I wish I could live in their house, right there near the cliffs. It must be so much fun to be able to see and hear the sea all the time. Yvette and I played with Charles. I love having a little two-year-old cousin. I think he adores me. He cried when we left.

Tuesday 4th July

They're at it again. War, war, war is all I hear. People seem obsessed by it. This morning it was Mr Masson and Mama. Mr Masson has been listening to the news broadcast on the wireless. He doesn't like the sound of what he's heard. Adolf Hitler is planning all sorts of things – he's building up his troops – he's threatening other countries. Why does he need to do that?

Mama wanted to know if Mr Hitler will invade France and Mr Masson said he hopes not. (So do I.) Mr Masson said he's thankful the boys aren't old enough to go to war, but he reckons that the government will be calling our people up to fight soon.

I ran to the hen house. I sat among my friends and told them how scared I am. Who is Adolf Hitler and what is he doing? I just hope he doesn't decide to come here.

Monday 10th July

Yvette and I went to Veules les Roses several times last week.
On Saturday, Uncle Thierry was at home. We all went to
the beach and had a picnic. We met some of Aunty Régine's
friends. They started on about Hitler and what he was up
to. All the adults seem to think that he's a real threat. Uncle
Thierry said he will go into the navy if they call him up to
fight because he's an engineer. I hope they don't, and I bet
Aunty Régine wouldn't want him to either.

Mama has started listening to the wireless (such a huge
ugly wooden thing there on the dresser). She sits with her ear
close to it and keeps telling us news about what Adolf Hitler
is doing. I'm sick of hearing his name!

Tuesday 1st August

I've been really busy. I've had a great month away from
school, cycling around and seeing friends. I've seen Georges

a few times, too, but I get tongue-tied when I see him. He's so good-looking he takes my breath away. I feel all silly and weak when we meet. I'm sure he thinks I'm pathetic.

Sebastien and I have been arguing a lot and Mama keeps warning us, so I've been trying to keep away from him, but it's not easy in such a small house. Yvette's mama is nice and she lets me go there often. I've been chatting to my hens, of course, and I visit Grandma nearly every day. Sebastien spends a lot of time over at the farm. Olivier Masson is his best friend. Olivier is fifteen, too, and he has two little sisters and a baby brother.

Sunday 6th August

Today, we went to St Valery en Caux for a family outing. It's a bit further along the coast and it's a bigger town than Veules les Roses. It's got a port full of fishing boats and a few private yachts. We watched the boats going in and out of the port. Papa promised that one day soon we can go out on one of those yachts, but then Mama went and spoiled it by saying, "Not if Adolf Hitler has anything to do with it." For once, Sebastien and I were thinking the same. We both told Mama not to be such an old misery!

Friday 11th August

Papa says the wheat is almost ripe. It will soon be harvest time. We'll all help. I'm looking forward to that.

Wednesday 16th August

The harvest started today. Everyone went, except Mama who had to stay and open and close the level-crossing gates. I couldn't believe it when she said she didn't mind. I suppose she thinks she can stay near the wireless and listen for news of Hitler!

I've had such a great day and now I'm so tired I can hardly keep my eyes open to write this. It was so hot and dusty, especially when Mr Masson and Papa and the other farm workers cut the wheat and threshed it. We all helped after that. Yvette and I got into a tangle trying to tie the stalks into bundles. We laughed so much we kept falling over each other. At lunchtime, we sat on the bundles of straw and ate bread and Camembert and salad and drank Grandma's apple juice.

Georges was there. He sat near me and smiled at me several times. It made me feel like I was floating on air. Is this what Grandma called being "in love"?

Wednesday 30th August

I can't believe the holidays are over so soon. The summer has flashed by. I've enjoyed it so much I want it to go on for ever, but lately things have been different in the village. Everyone looks worried, not full of the friendly smiles I'm used to. It's Adolf Hitler's fault.

I ran in from Yvette's this afternoon. Mama was listening to the wireless as usual. She put her finger to her lips, leaning closer to it. I knew it would be about Hitler. At last, she turned off the wireless and sighed. She told me he's built up a massive army in Germany. I think I knew that too, but it must be getting worse. Apparently, Hitler has ordered the German army to invade some other countries already. What a revolting man! He makes me sick. I feel a horrible tightness in my chest when I think about what he's doing. I wonder why Mr Daladier, our Prime Minister, doesn't do something to stop such a madman!

Sunday 3rd September

It's happened – what we all dreaded. I don't know quite what to think – it doesn't seem possible. It's now evening and the news still hasn't sunk in. It's been one of those days I'll never forget.

I spent the afternoon at Yvette's house, but as I cycled towards our house on my way home, I noticed Papa standing by the crossing gates. He was talking to a group of men, including Mr Masson. I wondered what was going on. I called to them as I arrived at our gateway. Several of them turned towards me, but none of them smiled, not even Papa. I thought somebody must have died. Papa hurried towards me. I could see tears in his eyes.

Then he told me. Adolf Hitler has invaded Poland. I asked what difference that makes and Mr Masson told me about an agreement that France and Great Britain have with Poland. If anyone attacks Poland, we have to stand up for them. So this morning, Mr Chamberlain, the British Prime Minister, declared war on Germany. And this afternoon, Mr Daladier did, too.

We're at war! The news made me feel so cold even

though it was a warm day. I folded my arms across my chest and hunched my shoulders against it. I shuddered. I'm still shivering now as I write about it. War! Up to now it has been all talk, but this is real. It's horrible. I'm scared about what's going to happen to us. Will people get killed, like in the last war? I don't really know much about the last war except that two of my uncles were killed. Their names are engraved on the memorial in the cemetery at the top of the hill.

I put my bicycle away and hurried to the hen house. I crouched down amongst the hens and told them about the terrible news. It didn't worry them. They're acting normally, as if nothing has changed.

Monday 4th September

Sebastien ran over from the farm this afternoon when I was in the hen house. His face was flushed and his eyes were wild. He gripped the wire of the hen run and peered through at me. Then he said that he and Olivier had been talking about the war. He sounded excited, not scared like me. What he said next really shocked me. They're going to volunteer to go and fight.

I pretended to laugh. I told him not to be so silly. He's not old enough, but he reckons he could lie. He is tall for his age and his voice has broken. He thinks they will take him in the army. I burst into tears. I couldn't help it. Sebastien is my brother, after all. He might be the most aggravating and frustrating brother on this earth, but he's the only one I've got!

I whispered that I couldn't bear it if he got himself killed like Papa's brothers that we never knew. I don't think Sebastien has ever wondered how Papa felt when his big brothers went away to fight and never came back. He stared at me. Then he made a joke about it, but I could see he was shaken. I stood up and gripped his fingers fiercely. I felt my brain spinning. I wanted to scream and shout, "Adolf Hitler's got to be stopped!"

Then we made a pact. I can't believe that this was me and Sebastien talking like this. We agreed that if anything happens here, we'll do everything we can together. We won't tell our parents because they'd say we're too young and they'd watch us like hawks. It will be our secret.

From now on, I'll have to keep this diary hidden. If Mama finds it, there'll be trouble. I think it will be a good idea to offer to clean my own room from now on. Then she won't ever be in here to find it. She'll be pleased with that. She's always complaining about how difficult it is to even get in here, let alone move around.

Monday 9th October

No news, except more about the German army, of course. It seems to be always on the move, threatening every country it can think of. Life goes on here as before (thank goodness). I go to school, learn English – which I still enjoy – see Yvette and Grandma and my hens. Sebastien and I are getting on fine. Mama can't believe it. I think she almost preferred it when we were rowing all the time. At least it gave her an excuse to moan at us.

I met Georges face to face outside school today and actually managed to say something. I can't remember what! I was so embarrassed that it took me half an hour to recover. I wish I wasn't so stupid. It's not as if I had never seen a boy before. We always have Sebastien's friends round. Apart from Olivier, there's Marcel Cariat and a couple of others. It's just that I'm not in love with any of them – only Georges.

Sunday 12th November

It's really strange. More than two months have passed since that day Britain and France declared war on Germany and sometimes I almost forget we're at war. Of course, I know about the fighting far away. How could I ever forget that? Mama always listens to the wireless.

Then, last night, we had a party in the village for the young men who are going into the army. Quite a few have signed up. I had a great time, dancing with Yvette. We were useless, tripping over each other's feet and giggling so much we almost fell over, like at the harvest. I know Georges was watching me. I sensed his eyes on me though I dared not look in his direction. I felt rather giddy and I couldn't help giggling even more.

But this morning we went to the Mayor's office to wave the young soldiers off. I didn't feel like laughing then. I had to bite my lip very hard to stop myself from bursting into tears. I kept thinking of Papa. As soon as he came in from work, I rushed over and gave him an enormous hug. He squeezed me tight and asked what he had done to deserve it. I felt embarrassed then, but I managed to whisper that I was glad he didn't have to go to war. He chuckled and kissed the top of my head. He said he's too old and that they only want to kill off the young ones. I heard a kind of bitterness in his voice. I snuggled against him. He has never said much about losing his brothers, but he must hurt deep down. I asked him if he thinks the fighting will reach here. He doesn't know. He thinks maybe Adolf Hitler will stop at nothing. I suppose he was being honest, but I don't like it – not one little bit.

Sunday 19th November

I'm miserable today. Uncle Thierry is going to join the navy. He doesn't want a farewell party, but I cycled over to Veules les Roses to see him. He said he'll be working in an engine room on a warship. I gulped. I hate the sound of that. It must be dark and noisy and smelly. And dangerous!

I looked at Aunty Régine. I could tell she'd been crying. Her eyes were red and her nose was swollen. She looked so miserable that it brought a lump to my throat. I kissed and hugged Uncle Thierry then I hurried outside to my bicycle and cried all the way home.

Monday 25th December 1939

Christmas Day has been very quiet! No one's in the mood for it. We all miss Uncle Thierry, especially Aunty Régine. He had been hoping to get home, but his fleet is always on stand-by, he said in his letter (he's not allowed to say where). There has been more fighting in other countries, but luckily there's no sign of it here. I hope it never reaches our region, I really do. I wonder if the soldiers have called a ceasefire today, like they did in the trenches of the last war.

Monday 1st January 1940

Happy New Year! I hope it will be a happy year, but I hate to think it probably won't be.

Thursday 11th January

The weather has turned bitterly cold. Everything is covered in a thick white blanket of snow. I haven't been to school this week. The water pipes have burst.

I woke up this morning and poked my nose out from under the covers. It was absolutely freezing – the worst day so far! I yanked the covers higher and peeped out over the top of them. Even though the shutters had been closed overnight I could make out leafy patterns of ice on my window.

Mama called up the ladder – time to get up and do my chores. I heard the back door slam then the clunk of the gates. I snuggled lower. Soon, the house shook as the train trundled by. I could tell it was a passenger train. Carriages don't clank as much as trucks! I heard Mama open the gates and come back indoors. She called again. I sighed and climbed out of bed, slipping quickly into my freezing clothes and shinning down the ladder. It was slightly warmer downstairs. I made myself some chocolate and sat by the stove, sipping the hot drink until I felt warmer. A few minutes later, I was dressed in my thick coat, hat, gloves, scarf and boots. As I opened the door to go out, I almost bumped into Olivier. His papa needed help with the animals. Mama said I could go when I had done my chores.

I took the eggs in then fetched a basket of logs for the stove. After that, Sebastien and I ran across the tracks. We found Papa and Olivier with Mr Masson in the barn. We were just in time to help deliver a lamb. It was so sweet. It gave me such a warm feeling inside.

Friday 26th January

Aunty Régine has had a letter from Uncle Thierry. It took three weeks to reach her and she has no idea where he is. She thinks he might be somewhere out in the Atlantic Ocean. That's such a long way away and so dangerous. She's very worried. I keep thinking of him stuck down in a warship's engine room. Poor Uncle Thierry – I hope there are no enemy submarines in that part of the ocean.

Monday 19th February

Something really thrilling happened today – to do with Sebastien and me. This morning, we listened to the wireless with Mama. It was all about the German army forcing its way across Europe. It made my whole body feel tensed up. I needed to get out. I hurried outside, grabbed my bicycle and pedalled off along the lane. The snow has gone at last, but it's still pretty cold. I rode fast, pushing my legs hard. I didn't notice where I was going, but slowly I felt more relaxed.

When I got back, Sebastien was out. He came in later, looking really excited. He told me he's joined a secret group with Marcel Cariat, who feels like we do about the German threat. Marcel's older brother, Patrice, formed the group and he's recruiting people they know feel the same. We've been hoping something like this would happen!

But Sebastien suddenly looked embarrassed. The Cariat brothers say I'm not old enough to join. I almost hit the ceiling. I am nearly fourteen! Sebastien agrees I should be in. There's going to be a meeting tomorrow night, and he's promised to take me with him, whatever they say. I'm so elated! I'm sworn to secrecy, of course!

Tuesday 20th February

I'm a girl of importance! I wish I could tell Yvette. Normally, I would have dashed straight round to her house, but I know that if I breathe a single word to her, it will prove to the Cariat brothers that I am too young after all.

I couldn't eat my dinner this evening. I guess it was nerves. I was relieved when at last Sebastien and I set off for the Cariats' house. Patrice frowned when he opened the door. He asked what I was doing there. He was rude about little sisters who blabbed. I was really proud of Sebastien. He stood up to Patrice. Marcel made a joke about me only blabbing to my chickens. I suppose he must have seen me in the hen house. In the end, Patrice shrugged and agreed I could join as long as I swore to secrecy. Of course, I did. So Patrice told us about the group – it's made up of people from Veules les Roses and our village and other villages around the area.

Then suddenly he turned to me. He actually smiled and said I might be useful, after all. Nobody in our village has a telephone so the group will need a messenger – and it's me! It's because of my bicycle. Patrice says everyone is used to seeing me cycling around so no one will suspect me. I can't wait to start. Mind you, it's scary too. It might be very dangerous.

Sunday 25th February

It's my birthday today! I had a new pen from Mama and Papa, which I am writing with now. It's good – no scratches or blots! Grandma gave me some lovely soft red gloves and a red scarf to match – very useful as it's still cold. Yvette came to dinner and we played some games. For once, we all forgot our thoughts of war.

Tuesday 19th March

There hasn't been a lot to write. It's exactly a month since I got excited about being a messenger and what have I done so far? Nothing! All I've done is go to school, as usual, learn English, as usual, feed my hens, as usual, visit Grandma, as usual, muck around with Yvette, as usual. It's so frustrating that I haven't had to do a single thing. No messages, nothing. (One good thing is that I've spoken to gorgeous Georges a few times – three, to be exact. I think he might like me.)

It's so hard not being allowed to tell Yvette about our group, but what is there to tell anyway? The war is still going on, but how can I be expected to stay interested if I'm not doing anything? Mama still tells us the news, but it all seems so far away. At least spring is coming and it's a lot warmer.

Friday 22nd March

Two days ago Mr Daladier resigned. I suppose he couldn't stand the strain of what's happening in Europe. Our new Prime Minister is Mr Reynaud. I hope he is strong enough to keep out the enemy.

Sunday 21st April

Another month has gone by. Hitler's armies are still marching all over the place and killing loads of people. Why can't someone stop him? I suppose he's too powerful. How can people get so much power?

The British are fighting against Hitler. Thousands of their soldiers are somewhere in Europe, but I'm not sure where. I don't talk about the war with any of my friends, only at home with Sebastien.

Friday 10th May

We've had a shock this evening. We were listening to the news broadcast on the wireless. The Germans have invaded Holland and Belgium. Belgium is next to France. That's such a frightening thought I couldn't help gripping Mama's arm. The French and British armies are fighting against them, but Hitler's army is so enormous, it seems as if it will never be defeated. Papa made it worse. He said, "If they've managed to invade our neighbours, what will stop him trying us?" It made my stomach turn over. The threat is growing nearer.

Saturday 11th May

Britain has a new Prime Minister, too. He's called Winston Churchill. Papa is pleased. He says he's a much stronger leader than Mr Chamberlain. Perhaps Mr Churchill will be able to stop Hitler doing any more damage.

Wednesday 15th May

I feel so sorry for the Dutch and Belgian people. I can't imagine how terrible it must be for them. They've had heavy bombing of their cities and there has been such fierce fighting. Today, we heard that Holland has surrendered to the Germans. I suppose they didn't have much choice.

I still haven't heard anything from Patrice. I'm feeling so frustrated. I want to be the one to stop Adolf Hitler! Sebastien says he hasn't heard anything either, but I'm suspicious. I think he's having secret meetings with Marcel and Patrice, but he won't admit it.

Today I cycled over to Yvette's house after school, but it's getting more and more difficult not being able to share my secret. I wish Yvette could be in our group, but I daren't mention it. I must keep quiet. Anyway, she never talks about the war or fighting or anything like that. That's where we seem to be different. She doesn't seem as worried as I am. She's more interested in homely things like cooking. She even enjoys helping her mama do the housework. I can't understand that. Yvette has been my friend since we were babies and we still sometimes cycle to Veules les Roses at the weekends and do all the usual things, but it almost seems like I've got more in common with my brother!

I'm finding it difficult to concentrate on my homework. The only subject I still like is English. I practise useful phrases on the hens. Then I try them on the family. Papa doesn't take me seriously and laughs at me. He sounds like Grandma. At least my teacher says I'm good! I want to become as good at English as her.

Thursday 23rd May

The news is dreadful! The German army has fought through the lines of French and British troops. The enemy has fought its way over the border from Belgium and is now in northeast France. Just think. They're in my country. I hoped they would never get here, but it's happened. Perhaps they will be defeated soon and the German army won't come this way. At the moment, they are battling their way towards the Channel near a place called Dunkerque. The British and French soldiers are being forced back towards the coast. They are heading into a dead end.

I asked Papa how far that is from here. It's only two or three hundred kilometres! Sebastien says the Germans might try to invade England. Perhaps if they do that, they won't bother to come along here.

Monday 27th May

This evening we heard some awful news on the wireless. Thousands of British and French soldiers are trapped on the beaches at Dunkerque. The German army is closing in on them. What will happen to them, poor things?

Tuesday 28th May

Belgium surrendered today, like the Dutch. I don't blame them. I suppose they couldn't stand being bullied by the German army any longer. I wonder what it's like to have the enemy taking over everything. I hope our government doesn't give in to the enemy! It's almost nine months since they declared war on Germany. Thank goodness there still hasn't been any fighting in our region.

Wednesday 29th May

I've waited and waited for messages from Patrice. Perhaps he only said I could be a messenger to keep me happy. Perhaps he never intended to use me. I'll try to find other ways to help without him.

The fighting is slowly creeping nearer. The German army has reached Abbeville. That's not far away at all!

Thursday 30th May

I'm finding it almost impossible to swallow my food. I'm so worried about what might happen to us. The news is that the German army is marching closer and closer. I wish this would all go away. I wish I could wake up and find it is all a nasty dream.

I just wish we could stop this war. I hate it! Why do people have to fight? Why do maniacs like Adolf Hitler have to try to take over the world?

Friday 31st May

At last – some action! This evening, Marcel Cariat knocked on the door. He pretended he wanted to borrow a book from Sebastien, but I sensed it was something else. Mama was in the room so he didn't say anything, but he kept glancing at me. My stomach began doing somersaults. I went out to the hen house and prowled around the pen, telling my hens about Marcel. They listened with their heads on one side.

I had only been there for a few minutes when Marcel and Sebastien strolled out into the garden. Marcel laughed when he saw where I was. I hurried out of the hen house. I felt so edgy, I thought I would burst. But I was right. Early tomorrow morning, I have to take a message from Patrice to Veules les Roses!

Marcel has given me instructions. I've got to go to the Rue Victor Hugo. I know it. It's quite near Aunty Régine's house. I have to find number 12 – it's a little cottage quite close to the sea and has a black front door. I have to knock once and wait. A person called Hélène will come to the door. The message is for her alone.

Now for the even more exciting bit – I've got a coded message to say first! I have to say, "How are the flowers in your garden?" and she will reply, "The red ones are the most beautiful." Then I have to give her the message.

Marcel handed me a small envelope and I tucked it in the pocket of my skirt. It's under my pillow now, waiting till tomorrow. Marcel asked me if I was up to the job, but when he saw the expression on my face, he didn't want an answer!

I've got this kind of thrill running through me. It won't go away. How will I ever sleep tonight? This is what I've been waiting for ever since we knew we were at war. It's the real thing!

Saturday 1st June
Morning

I hardly slept. I've got up and dressed very early. I'm so nervous. If I creep down the ladder, perhaps they won't notice me going out. Then I can get to Veules les Roses and back before they wonder where I am.

Midday

I've done it! I crept down the ladder and hurried to fetch my bicycle. I was wheeling it round the side of the house when Mama came out of the door. She made me jump and I was sure she could tell there was a letter in my pocket. She wanted to know where I was going. I almost panicked. An idea popped into my head. I said I thought I'd go and see Aunty Régine because she must miss Uncle Thierry. I asked if I could take her a few eggs. Mama thought that was a good idea. But that was an awkward moment.

Mama wrapped four eggs in paper and I placed them in my cycle basket. Then I rode away up the slope. I met nobody as I sped along the lanes towards Veules les Roses. I delved into my pocket loads of times to check that the letter was still there. My hand was shaking. As I approached Veules les Roses, I realized my legs were shaking too. Supposing Hélène wasn't there?

I pedalled along the main street, the Rue Victor Hugo. I rode slowly, looking for number 12, the house that Marcel had described. I was almost at the sea when, at last, I found the little run-down cottage with the black front door. Trembling all over, I leant my bicycle against the wall and walked up to the door. Before I could knock, the door opened a few centimetres. Quickly, I stepped back. Then I heard a very quiet shaky voice and the face of an old woman appeared in the narrow opening.

She asked if I had come to see her. I was suspicious. I didn't think this could be Hélène. I was expecting a younger woman. I could hardly stand there for shaking. My mouth felt incredibly dry, but I licked my lips and whispered, "How are the flowers in your garden?"

She didn't hear me at first and I had to repeat it. I held my breath, waiting to see if she was the right person. She gave me the answer I needed, and I felt the air rushing out of my lungs like the steam from a train. I felt a bit dizzy. My brain was spinning, but I was delighted. The coded message had worked!

A shrivelled, rather knobbly hand reached out towards me. I was really amazed that this old woman was Hélène. She asked me if I had a message from Patrice. I put my hand in my pocket, but she told me to wait. She opened the door a little wider. I wasn't sure if I should step into the old lady's house. You never know who to trust, but then I remembered that she had said the password so she must be all right, and I took a step forward. She grabbed my arm. Her fingers reminded me of birds' claws. She pulled me into the dark cottage. When I took out the letter, she snatched it immediately.

She opened the envelope and peered at the letter. She smiled at me and told me it was a dummy run just to see if I could do the job. She said I'd done well, and she wrote me a quick note to take back to Patrice. Then she told me she thought they might need me again soon.

I was still shaking a few minutes later as I climbed the hill to my aunt's house, high above the village, with a new letter in my pocket. But I forgot everything else when I saw Aunty Régine's face. She'd been crying. I put the eggs on the kitchen table, then kissed Aunty Régine and picked up Charles and gave him a big hug. She stood at the window, staring out to sea. She misses Uncle Thierry so much. She showed me another letter she has had from him.

I stood beside her. The sea looked so calm and harmless and peaceful. It's difficult to believe that there are many warships out there, trying to defend France. I thought about

Uncle Thierry. He's such great fun and I've missed seeing him since he went into the navy. I swallowed hard and said I hoped the war would be over very soon, and I expect the ships are solid. I don't know if that helped. Aunty Régine says she tries to be strong for little Charles's sake.

I couldn't relax. My hand kept straying to the letter inside my pocket. At last, I left her house and cycled away from the sea. I hurried straight home, as I was instructed. Now I'm waiting for Marcel to come.

Afternoon

I saw Marcel coming down the lane just after I had finished writing in my diary. He was holding Sebastien's book. I went out to meet him. I nodded and grinned, but said nothing. He nodded back and held the book out to me. I took it and quickly slipped the letter into his hand. I went indoors, feeling pleased with myself. My first official mission has been a success.

Sunday 2nd June

What a day! I'm feeling really good about everything. Well, except one thing, but more about that later.

I was cycling home today when I met an old man from the village. He started chatting about my red bicycle. He always sees me speeding around, he said. I'm famous! I was pleased. That was exactly what Patrice Cariat said all those months ago. Then the old man said he had seen refugees on the main road towards Veules les Roses. They've had to flee because the Germans have taken over their towns.

It was so hot and the sky was quite dark, but I headed towards Veules les Roses. I wanted to see for myself. As I came to the brow of the hill and looked down on the road I saw a long column of women and children and old people. There seemed to be hundreds of them. Some were dragging handcarts piled high with their belongings, but most of them had nothing but what they were carrying. Some were limping and I could hear children crying. They all looked so miserable that I wanted to cry, too.

I bit my lip and pedalled down amongst them. I spoke to a girl who looked about the same age as me. I told her my name as I dropped my bicycle at the roadside. The girl burst into tears. I put my arm round her then she managed to tell me what had happened. She's called Anais Leclerc and she lives north of Abbeville. Two days ago, the Germans came with tanks and now their house is in ruins. They ran away, but they have no idea where they are going. I can't imagine how terrible that must be.

Anais told me they've slept rough for the past two nights. They've had no food and they've been drinking any water they could find. I met her mama, who was carrying a little boy. She looked exhausted and her eyes were so sad.

There was a flash of lightning. It must have been the lightning that sprang me into action. Never mind Patrice. I decided to do this on my own. I leapt on my bicycle, telling them to wait here. I would see what I could do. I'd had an idea.

I raced along the lanes, back to the village. Mama was at the level-crossing gate. A train had just gone through. I shouted, and Mama looked up. I stood astride my bicycle as there was another flash. I was out of breath, but I had to tell Mama everything as fast as I could. Mama frowned. She said, "You can't make a feast appear like magic!"

Sebastien and Olivier came out of the house. I repeated my story even faster. I finished by suggesting that the people could sleep in Mr Masson's barn while we went round the village collecting food. Sebastien smiled at me and I smiled back. That felt good.

The boys set off at once to ask Olivier's papa. I hoped that the two of them would manage to persuade Mr Masson. Mama wanted to know how many people there were. Then she said, "We can't let fellow human beings suffer." I hugged her quickly then followed the boys to the farm. The sky was jet black. Flashes of lightning streaked across the dark clouds and thunder rumbled noisily. Sebastien and Olivier had found Mr Masson in the barn. Mrs Masson was there, too, with Olivier's little brother and two little sisters.

Mrs Masson is marvellous! She persuaded Mr Masson to say "yes", but he's only allowing them to stay for one night. I thanked him as I whizzed off again on my bicycle. By the time I reached the main road, big spots of rain had begun to fall. I found that a lot of the people had moved on, but Anais and about forty others were sheltering under the trees that lined the road.

I waved and shouted the good news against the noise of the wind that was whirling through the trees. We stayed under the trees while the worst of the storm passed. We were all very bedraggled as we set off along the lane to the village.

They are safely in Mr Masson's barn now.

Later

I'm so tired I don't know how I climbed the ladder tonight.
It's late and I've had the busiest evening of my life! But I'll
have to stay awake. There's so much more to write. When I
had left the refugees in the barn, I hurried to Yvette's house.
I knew that she would want to help collect food for the
refugees. As soon as she heard about them she rushed out
to fetch her bicycle. Then Olivier and Sebastien covered one
half of the village while Yvette and I did the other. At each
house, I explained what we wanted and smiled in my most
pleasing way so that most people gave me something.

My heart was fluttering as I rode up to Georges Dubois's
house. I felt myself blush when Georges opened the door. I
muttered and shuffled my feet. I couldn't look him in the
eye. My mouth felt dry and I had difficulty thinking what
to say. In the end I mumbled something about refugees and
about them being hungry. I don't know what I was expecting
from him, but not the sharp voice telling me that the people
were only gypsies, out to see what they could get.

I was stunned. I glanced up. An ugly sneer transformed
his handsome face as he told me how much he admired the

Germans because they are such a strong nation. He even said we should be strong like them. He didn't believe all the "lies" about their cruelty. He had the nerve to tell me I didn't understand and that I'm just a weak sentimental female!

I was disgusted. How could he think like that? How could I ever have imagined I was in love with him? I turned away and cycled madly along to the next house, seething. I had to call on quite a few friendly villagers before I could get rid of my anger and put thoughts of Georges right out of my head. Soon my cycle basket was full of cheese and bread, fruit and salad. It was growing dark, and I was beginning to feel tired, but I kept going. I made several deliveries to the barn.

News had got round. When I arrived at Grandma's house, I could smell soup cooking. I looked at the huge pan on the stove and hugged Grandma. She's a marvel! She told me what a good girl I am to help the refugees. She agreed how terrible it must be to lose your home like that! The pot of soup was so big she said I was to send Papa to fetch it. After another hug, I was on my way again, collecting food and delivering it to the barn. Some villagers gave me clothes, too.

On my final visit to the barn, I shared some of Grandma's delicious soup with Anais and her mama. Mrs Leclerc had tears in her eyes as she told me that her husband is in the army. They don't know where he is, or even if he's still alive.

I didn't know what to say so I finished my soup in silence. I couldn't help a guilty feeling creeping into my mind. Why have they lost so much, while I still have everything?

Monday 3rd June

They've gone! The train whistle woke me up this morning. The sun was shining brightly through the slats in the shutters. My first thought was about Georges. I hadn't got over the shock of his words. I hate him now instead of thinking I loved him! Then I remembered the refugees. I dressed quickly, snatched a hunk of bread from the kitchen and ran across the railway line towards the farm. But when I arrived at the barn it was empty. I sat down on a bale of straw and cried. They hadn't even said goodbye. After a few moments, I hurried to the farmhouse.

Mrs Masson was in the kitchen. She told me that they had gone at first light. She said some nice things about how kind I had been, but that didn't help much. I felt so disappointed. But then she handed me a sheet of paper. It was a note from Anais. I felt better immediately as I unfolded the paper and read. It said:

Dear Sophie,

You will be my friend for life, even though we may never meet again. We all feel so much better for the food and shelter you arranged for us. We are heading west, in the hope that we might find somewhere to stay, away from the fighting. Please thank your brother and your friends and all those people who gave us food, especially the old lady who made that delicious soup!

I hope the war is soon over so that we can all start to build our lives again. Pray for my papa, wherever he is.

Grosses bises,

Anais Leclerc

I hope they'll be all right. I wonder if I'll ever hear from Anais again.

Tuesday 4th June

There are more refugees on the main road every day. I'd love to help them all, but know that's impossible. Mama says we can't feed the whole of France. I suppose she's right. We ought to save as much food as we can in case we need it ourselves.

Wednesday 5th June

Those British and French soldiers we heard about last week – the ones that were trapped on the beaches at Dunkerque – well, we've heard that loads have been rescued by warships and hundreds of little boats that made the journey over the sea from England, but thousands more soldiers have been killed or taken prisoner. I asked Papa what happens to the captured ones. He said they'll be kept in prisoner-of-war camps until the end of the war and there will be many more casualties and prisoners before it's all over.

War is so ghastly!

Patrice says that some British soldiers are moving this way. Perhaps they'll be able to look after us. I think Mama is trying to put on a brave face for my sake. I'm sure she's really as scared as I am. If both sides keep on coming, we might be stuck right in the middle! They'll be fighting right here in our village!

Thursday 6th June

It's been such a hectic and exciting day! How will I ever forget such surprising events? It's lunchtime now and I've snatched a few minutes to run home and write in my diary. We haven't been to school, for obvious reasons! We had just eaten our breakfast this morning when we heard a strange sound in the distance. It was like a wailing animal mixed with a deep miserable groan. I had no idea what it could be. Sebastien and I dashed out and raced up the lane to the corner.

I couldn't believe my eyes. A long line of soldiers in khaki uniforms was marching into the village, but at their head was a man wearing a skirt. That man was holding a strange instrument in front of him. He had some kind of bag under his arm and he was blowing into a pipe, which was making the terrible sound. I've never seen or heard anything so weird in all my life!

Sebastien ran towards the soldiers. He called over his shoulder that they were British. I ran behind him and joined the group of people watching from the grassy bank at the corner. Grandma was there. I stood next to her, panting hard. Grandma was thrilled. She thought my English would be useful after all. Then Yvette ran over to join us. She held her hands over her ears and laughed. She dared me to go and speak to the soldiers as I'm best in the class. I grinned at her and nodded. I began to tingle all over. It was so exciting! This seemed like a chance to show them all how well I can speak English!

Suddenly, the strange instrument gave a loud whine then a gasp. Then it shuddered and was silent. I stared at the man with the instrument and asked Sebastien why an Englishman would wear a skirt like that. He laughed and told me it isn't a skirt. It's called a kilt. He said they're not English, they're Scottish. And the strange instrument is called a bagpipe. He's so clever, my brother!

I took a closer look at the soldiers. Some had bandages round their heads, some had arms in slings and others had crutches to help them along. They all looked bedraggled and many looked utterly miserable.

Their officer stepped forward and shouted to the crowd, "*Parlez-vous anglais?*" He had a weird accent and it sounded really funny. I held back for a moment, though my heart was racing. I felt Yvette nudging me. Suddenly, Grandma waved to the soldiers. She pointed at me and called, "*Oui, ma petite-fille, Sophie, parle anglais.*" I felt my face redden. I was furious with Grandma, but I was secretly pleased, too.

I felt Sebastien's hand on my back and suddenly, I was running down the bank and standing facing the officer.

I tried really hard and told him I speak a little English, but my face was burning like a forest fire. He asked me my name and I told him – "My name is Sophie Ridel." I was really pleased that I had understood his question. I said, "I am fourteen years old."

He told me that he's called Captain Mackenzie. After that he spoke so fast I had no idea what he said. I shrugged my shoulders and shook my head. The officer rubbed his stomach then pointed into his mouth. They were hungry. He pretended to yawn. They were tired, too.

I beamed at him. I remembered how easy it had been to feed the refugees and find them somewhere to sleep. Somehow or other I managed to tell him that we would help. I asked Sebastien if he thought Mr Masson would let them stay in the barn. Sebastien ran to the farm to find out.

There's so much to write. I'll try and carry on tonight.

Evening

I tried my hardest to explain to Captain Mackenzie about the barn and the food that we would collect. I can see now that my English isn't very good at all, but I did my best. Luckily, Sebastien wasn't long in coming back. Olivier was with him

49

and I could see old Mr Duval, the Mayor, a short way behind, hobbling along with his walking stick. Sebastien brought good news. Mr Masson said yes. So the next thing was to persuade everyone to donate food again. Yvette promised to fetch some from her mama. Grandma hurried away to make some more soup. She made us all laugh when she asked if we thought the foreigners would like French soup.

Mr Duval was hot and bothered. His face was red and he leant on his stick while he got his breath back. I felt very important as I introduced him to Captain Mackenzie. The officer saluted and Mr Duval bowed and apologized for not being there sooner. They didn't understand a word of what each other said so I was kept busy trying to translate. It wasn't easy! The Captain asked if there was a doctor in the village. He looked sad when he told us his army doctor had been killed by the Germans.

Mr Duval sent Yvette to fetch Dr Lambert. Then Marcel walked over to me. He told me there would be another message to take to Hélène tomorrow. It didn't seem fair. Instead of no action at all, now I was needed in two places at once.

Suddenly, I noticed Georges Dubois standing watching us. I coughed. Luckily, Marcel took the hint and walked over to his friends. A few moments later he strolled casually towards Georges. I heard what they said. Marcel talked about the soldiers. He asked Georges if he was excited to see them. I know he was sounding Georges out to find out whose side he was on. Georges scowled at Marcel as he told him he didn't like the British soldiers. He doesn't want them here. When Marcel pointed out that the German army is getting closer, Georges turned and walked away. When Georges was out of earshot I warned Marcel about him. Then the soldiers went to the barn.

We've worked so hard today and now it's late. All I want to do now is sleep.

Friday 7th June
8 am

Marcel has just arrived. I heard his voice downstairs. I guess it's time to go to Veules les Roses. We had a message last night that school has been cancelled for the time being. I don't know whether I'm happy or sad about that. I like school, but I think I'm going to be kept busy here.

Midday

This morning I thought I was going to die! My writing is rather wobbly because I'm still shaking now. If this is war, I wish it had never started and I hope it finishes very soon. This is what happened.

I climbed down the ladder and said hello to Marcel. When we were sure Mama wasn't looking, he gave me another letter. I shoved it into my pocket. I promised to be as quick as I could, fetched my bicycle and set off. Veules les Roses is only a few kilometres away, so I hoped I wouldn't be long.

In no time at all, I was knocking on the old door in Rue Victor Hugo. As soon as the door opened a crack, I slipped inside. Hélène slit open the envelope and read the letter. She told me it said that the British are here and that the enemy is closing in. She said she would make preparations there in Veules les Roses, in case the soldiers can't stop them. Then she thanked me and said there was no reply.

I didn't have time to visit Aunty Régine. I knew I would be needed in the village. Even if they didn't need me to translate, there was food to collect.

I'm all of a quiver as I write this – I can hardly bear to recall it. I was halfway home when I heard the sound of aircraft. I stopped and looked behind me. There were two low-flying planes heading straight towards me. For a few seconds, I watched them as they came nearer and nearer. Why were they flying so low? Were they French planes? Or British? Or were they German?

Just in time, I threw myself into the ditch at the side of the road. There was a sudden deafening burst of gunfire. I heard a rain of bullets hit the road where I had been only a few seconds before. The planes roared overhead, skimming the bushes, but I had seen the black cross on the wings. They must be German.

The shock of what had happened hit me like a punch in the stomach. They had tried to kill me! I had to fight for breath. It felt as if someone had tied a belt round my body and was pulling it tight. I couldn't move for several minutes. Then all I wanted was to be back in the village. I made myself move.

Feeling very shaky, I climbed out of the ditch and picked up my bicycle. A really scary thought kept going round and round in my head. *They were trying to kill me!* But what were those planes doing around here? I guess there's only one answer. They were on the look-out for British or French soldiers.

I had to get back to the village to warn everyone, but I had no energy in my legs. The wind seemed against me and the journey that was usually so easy felt like climbing a mountain peak. And I had to stay alert, looking and listening in case those planes came back.

It felt like ages before I was free-wheeling down the hill into the village. All the streets were empty and silent.

Instead of rushing to the barn, I've climbed up here, into the safety of my bedroom. I think I might stay at home for the rest of the day. I'll go and see my hens. They'll help me to get over my first real experience of war.

Evening

I feel a bit better now. I didn't stay at home, after all. I've been over to the barn. It was bursting with soldiers and people helping them. I couldn't see anyone I knew at first. Then I saw Yvette with Dr Lambert. She was bandaging a soldier's head and she waved to me, so I pushed through the crowds of men to reach her. I know what she wants to do when she leaves school. She's going to be a nurse, and I'm sure she'll be an excellent one. As I talked to her I could hear a quaking in my voice – I still haven't fully recovered – but

Yvette didn't seem to notice. She was already moving on to the next patient.

I saw Captain Mackenzie over in the far corner. He was trying to talk to Mr Duval, but they were both shrugging their shoulders and waving their hands. It was obvious they didn't understand each other. I managed to reach them. I asked Mr Duval if two planes flew low over here this morning and he said they had. They were German Stukas. Luckily, everyone was inside the barn when they flew over so they can't have seen the soldiers. That's a relief, anyway.

I told him about my narrow escape then I tried to tell my story to Captain Mackenzie, in English. A frown spread across his face. Apparently some of his men had been killed by Stukas a few days ago. I asked him why he had come to this part of France, but I couldn't understand any of his reply. It's becoming more and more obvious how little English I know. I felt tearful and turned away. Mr Duval must have noticed. He patted my arm and told me I was doing very well. I don't think he realized quite how shaken I felt. I wished Mrs Ferrand, my English teacher, was there.

At that moment, my wish was granted. I saw Mrs Ferrand pushing through the crowds. Someone must have gone to fetch her. I felt stronger as I introduced her to the Scottish Captain. It helped me recover a little. Mrs Ferrand listened to the Captain then translated everything for Mr Duval. She learned that the Scottish soldiers are part of the 51st

Highland Division. They were at Dunkerque, but instead of being evacuated like many of the other British soldiers they were ordered to move on to this region. They've been fighting in the Somme valley. Now they're here to guard the railway – to make sure the Germans don't take it over – and also to protect the sugar factory.

At that moment, I caught sight of Marcel. He was heading my way. As he passed by, I whispered, "No message." I smiled to myself. No one had noticed. I felt like a real spy! But I had no time to think about that. I joined the others who were collecting food. Then I headed home. Mama was by the crossing gates. She says she doesn't mind missing all the action. (I wouldn't have minded missing a certain part of it!) I didn't tell her about my trip to Veules les Roses or the Stukas.

Late

This evening, I saw a single line of soldiers marching over from the barn. They reached the railway line and began to take up positions along the track. One soldier remained at the barriers. I noticed his dark brown hair, pale freckly face and bright blue eyes. I thought he looked very young.

Mama went back indoors, but I decided to visit the chickens. I fed them with grain and collected several eggs. I felt the young soldier's eyes watching me. As I took the eggs to the house, I smiled at him. I told him my name and asked him for his. He's called Angus Brown. Then I told him my age. He's eighteen.

I can't help thinking about Sebastien. He's sixteen now, only two years younger than Angus. In only two years' time, Sebastien might have to go and fight! I hope the war will be over by then.

I watched Angus for a moment as he walked up and down with his rifle over his shoulder. The grey circles round his eyes made him look tired and ill. I wonder what he's experienced since he's been in France. So far, I thought I was doing quite well speaking English with him, but when I asked him if he was hungry, I had a bit of a problem. He said, "Aye." I didn't understand. Then he told me it's a Scottish word for "Yes" – it's all too complicated.

He flashed me a smile and his eyes twinkled. When he did that I realized he's rather good-looking. I ran indoors, cut a chunk of bread and a piece of cheese, and ran back outside with the food for Angus.

Saturday 8th June
Midday

This morning, I've been fetching more food from the villagers. They weren't as generous as when we fed the refugees. They say they might need the food for themselves if things get worse. Then I went to the barn and helped as much as I could with the wounded soldiers. Several times, I heard German aircraft flying low over the village.

I'm shaking again as I write this. Why? Well, a little while ago, I thought I heard a rumble of thunder. Papa said it isn't thunder. It's gunfire! It's in the distance, but I keep imagining it's getting nearer. I'm keeping my fingers crossed that it isn't. Oh dear! What will we do?

I was really pleased to see Angus on duty again. I went to talk to him. I wanted to try out my English and find out more about him. I discovered that he speaks a bit of French. Between us, we managed to communicate. He lives in Scotland, in the mountains, in a town called Inverness – I think that's how you spell it. He told me he misses his home terribly. His eyes looked very sad when he said that. Then he told me about his parents and his sister. Her name is Morag and she's fourteen years old, too.

Angus thinks I ask a lot of questions, but he doesn't seem to mind. He's right. I'm inquisitive. I want to know everything about him. He doesn't like being a soldier and he doesn't want to fight, but he had no choice. All the boys of his age had to go to war. Just like our boys, I suppose. He asked me about my family. I told him about my hens, too, and how much I love them. And he didn't laugh. He seemed to understand. I'm beginning to realize that I like Angus! He's gone off duty now.

I'm feeling very restless. I'm lying on my bed listening to the heavy guns in the distance. How far away are they? Not many kilometres, I guess.

Afternoon

The trains that have rumbled in today are full of British and French soldiers. Other troops are arriving by lorry or on foot. Why are they all coming here? I went into the village. I just had to see what was going on. I'll admit it was also an excuse to see Angus again. I cycled around the village, looking for him, but there was no sign of him anywhere. I stopped by a group of Scottish soldiers and asked them. I wish I hadn't. They all laughed. I understood enough of what they said to know that they were joking about Angus finding a French girlfriend already. I hurried away, blushing scarlet.

I wonder where Angus is.

I watched other soldiers preparing their guns. I'm sure I got in everyone's way. Soldiers filled the village. Apart from their rifles, they had machine guns, which they set up on the southern side of the village.

Then a French motorcycle messenger sped into the village. Quickly, news spread that the Germans are not far away. They're flattening everything in their path. They've got tanks and other heavy weapons. Can nothing stop the German war machine?

Suddenly, I was scared. I wanted to be with Mama, but I was nearly back at the house when I heard a shout behind me. It was Marcel. I'd got to take a message. Patrice hadn't had time to write a note so I had to memorize it. I repeated the message several times to make sure I had got it right.

When Marcel had gone, I found myself speeding along the road to Veules les Roses. The wind blew my fear away. It was so exciting to be delivering such an urgent message. I recited the message to myself in time with my knees as they pumped up and down. I arrived breathless at Hélène's house.

I was panting heavily as I recited the message. Hélène was to hide all her papers, burn evidence and warn other friends, then she must prepare for the worst as the enemy is not far off.

I couldn't believe I was saying this. It didn't feel real, more like acting in a play. I think that's what helped me cope with it.

The old lady was so calm. She thanked me. I was to tell Patrice that all the secrets are safe with her. She'll give nothing away, even under torture. She's sure the Germans will not suspect her. They'll think she's too old. Then she told me to go.

I didn't need telling a second time! My legs worked up and down like pistons. I desperately wanted to get back home before there was any fighting in the village. I thought about Hélène's words, "even under torture". It made shivers shoot up and down my spine. I had learned in history lessons about torture that took place a long time ago. Surely that doesn't still happen nowadays?

I was nearly home. I could hear sounds of guns firing over in Mr Masson's fields on the other side of the village. I saw French and Scottish soldiers everywhere, hidden in ditches, in position at corners, manning machine guns, but there was no sign of the enemy. I dodged between the jeeps and trucks and soldiers and weapons that clogged the road and sped directly to Patrice's house, dropped my bicycle at the gate and ran up the path. Patrice must have seen me coming. He opened a window and leaned out. I repeated Hélène's message, almost word for word, then before Patrice could reply, I had turned and was running for the gate.

I arrived home just as the first shell whistled through the air. I dived in through the doorway as the explosion rocked the house. I ran to the window and saw a huge cloud of smoke rising into the sky. The shell had landed only a couple of hundred metres away. Mama looked deathly white and she was shaking all over. I found that I was shaking, too. I can hardly hold my pen to write this.

Later

I'm still shaking. I'm so scared I can hardly keep still, let alone write. It's been going on for hours.

I'm glad Papa and Sebastien got back safely from the farm just after that first shell. It had landed quite near Yvette's house. I'm so desperately worried. Yvette, dear kind Yvette. Please let her be all right. Please don't let anyone get hurt or killed. As I huddled in a corner I thought about poor Grandma, all on her own in her house near the church. She must be frightened out of her wits!

A second shell whistled and exploded somewhere near the first one. Mama and I clung to each other as the deafening sound of gunfire sounded across the village. Then we heard another shell whistling through the air. This one sounded nearer. We all flattened ourselves on the cold stone floor. The windows rattled loudly as the shell exploded.

Mama shrieked, "We have to close the shutters!" She started clambering up the ladder. I followed her. Before closing my bedroom shutters I stared out across the farmyard to the village. Black smoke and flames billowed out from one of the houses and an old shed, but it looked as if Grandma's and Yvette's houses were undamaged.

Suddenly, I saw a huge German tank trundling into the village. I screamed. Mama hurried over and stood beside me at the window. She put her hands to her mouth as I pointed. There were German soldiers, too, running beside the tank, firing their rifles. It was horrible. I was terrified. Yet it seemed so unreal, almost as if I was watching a film like the one I had seen once at the Picture Palace in Rouen. But it was also so real, here, in my own village.

We quickly closed the shutters and climbed back down the ladder. No one spoke after that. We all sat in the living room, waiting, listening to the booms and bangs and the constant rat-a-tat of the machine guns. The room was almost dark with the shutters closed and when the next shell landed, the house shook as much as before, but the windows didn't rattle so loudly. Then we heard the aircraft.

Sebastien said it sounded heavier than the ones that came over yesterday. It did. It was a very loud drone. Papa said it was a bomber! A bomber? I thought I was scared before. But now – I was petrified. We were all going to be killed! I moved closer to Papa. I could feel the tension in his body as he pulled me into his arms. Suddenly, there was a different kind of noise, like a rush of wind. We all threw ourselves on the floor. It was a bomb! I held my breath. A second later, there was a massive explosion. The shutters rattled noisily and the ground shook. The enemy had dropped a bomb on our village!

Papa gripped me so tightly I felt crushed, but I didn't want to move. I was totally tensed up, waiting for more bombs to fall. But the drone of the aircraft faded, leaving the everlasting noise of machine guns, rifles and tanks. After a while, Papa gently pushed me away from him and stood up.

My body began to relax a little, but so many questions rushed into my brain. Where had the bomb landed? We had survived it, but how many people had it killed? I was terrified for Grandma, all alone in her house. I prayed the bomb hadn't landed anywhere near her, but it was impossible to find out if she was all right. Nobody could go outside while bullets were flying.

For ages, we all had to stay in the house. I felt twitchy and restless. I hated being cooped up like this. Besides worrying about the people of the village, I was desperately anxious about the hens. They were cooped up, too. The poor things must be petrified out there with all the noise and no shutters to close. I wished I could go and comfort them. But I knew there was nothing I could do. We just had to wait until this was over.

Very late

It's getting dark. They're still fighting outside. I think it's going to keep on forever. I'm lying on my bed, using a torch to write by. Mama and Papa don't know I'm writing this, of course. They told me and Sebastien to try and sleep. As if we could! Every so often, I peep through cracks in the shutters, but I can't see much. I hold my breath each time I hear a shell and hope that no one in the village will be hurt. I listen to the gunfire and keep thinking about Grandma and Yvette and the soldiers out there fighting, especially Angus Brown. How many of the soldiers will be killed? Will we all survive?

Sunday 9th June
6 am

I don't know what time it stopped. I must have fallen asleep eventually with my diary and pencil in my hands because when I woke up that was the first thing I noticed. The second thing was the quiet. I listened. Silence!

I've just climbed out of bed and opened the shutter a little way. There's no sign of the tanks. The soldiers have all gone, but I'm sure I can see some bodies lying on the ground. Are they dead? I'm going to wake the others up.

10 am

After I had hidden my diary, I called Mama and Papa and Sebastien. We all dressed very quickly, shinned down the ladder and hurried outside. First, we had to go and see if Grandma was all right.

I was stunned by what I saw as we ran through the village.

It had been such a quiet peaceful place until a few hours ago. Now it was torn to pieces. Burnt-out vehicles littered the road and several houses had been flattened and many damaged.

And the bodies! My stomach felt as if it had been gripped by a giant claw. I covered my eyes as we passed through. I couldn't bear to look. There were quite a lot of people around – people carrying the dead and wounded, Dr Lambert walking amongst the bodies, Mr Duval hobbling about, muttering, his old face as grey as stone. I heard that they had set up a temporary hospital for the wounded in the village hall. The dead were being taken to the Mayor's office.

I wondered about Angus. What had happened to him?

We reached Yvette's house. Some of the shutters were damaged and a few slates were missing from the roof, but I was so relieved when she ran out to the gate as we went by. I hugged her. She was very pale and she didn't smile. She looked absolutely terrified.

But we didn't stop. We had to check that Grandma was all right. I sprinted ahead. As I came round the bend near her house, I screamed. Grandma's house had several broken windows and there was a hole in one corner of the wall, but it was the church I was staring at – or the space where the church had been. It was just a pile of rubble. That bomb – it must have been a direct hit. It was terrible, but at least it had missed Grandma!

We all ran towards her house. Grandma opened the door

as we hurried up the path. She was covered in dust and bits of plaster, but otherwise she was unharmed. I burst into tears. I was so relieved. I brushed away some of the dirt on her clothes and she gently told me not to fuss. She smiled and said that she was fine. She told us that when the tanks came she just lay on the floor underneath the kitchen table and prayed. She said it would take more than a few Germans to put an end to her! She spat on the ground in disgust.

I hugged her. Good old Grandma!

As soon as I knew that she was safe, I hurried back home. I wanted to know how the chickens were. I opened the pen and went in. I was amazed. They met me in the normal way, as if nothing unusual had happened. They fussed around me as I threw them a few handfuls of grain, and muttered away as they scratched in the soil. I do love the way they manage to cope with everything. They're so brilliant and ridiculous!

I started to giggle and that turned into a laugh. Then I was sobbing. I couldn't stop. I must have been there for quite a while, but eventually I sat down on the edge of the feeding trough and wiped my eyes. Several hens stopped to look up at me then carried on as before. They seemed to have coped better than the humans! They had even managed to lay some eggs!

After a few more minutes with the hens, I ran back to Grandma's. The others had already set about clearing up the mess. I took Grandma's mat outside and began to shake it. We swept and cleaned for about an hour then we came home.

I always seem to feel tired lately. The whole world is turned upside down.

Midday

I can't believe it. Marcel has just been here. I've got to go to Veules les Roses. I don't know if I'm brave enough to go.

Afternoon

I did go. I made myself. We're at war. Sebastien and I promised we'd do what we can, so this is what I have to do.

It's a warm, sunny Sunday. Papa was over at Mr Masson's farm and Mama was on duty at the level-crossing gates so it was easy for me to sneak to the shed to fetch my bicycle. I found Sebastien pumping up his tyres. I told him where I was going then I instructed him to cover for me. If Mama or Papa asked where I'd gone, he had to say I was visiting Aunty Régine. And if I got into any difficulties, I told him I'd go there anyway.

I was amazed at his reaction. He actually told me to take care. Then I was bowled over by what he said next. He thinks I'm very brave. His words gave me a warm feeling inside. I smiled and gently pushed his arm. I told him he's brave, too. I let on that I know he's been out and about with Marcel and Patrice. He opened his mouth to speak, but I stopped him. It's best I know as little as possible.

I met nobody as I pedalled along the lanes, although I could hear gunfire in the distance. The fighting had moved towards the west. I had Patrice's message safely in my head again. This time I felt more confident about it and I wasn't worried about forgetting it before I reached Hélène. The message was about the soldiers who had fought in the village the day before, including Angus Brown, of course.

In spite of what Sebastien had said, I didn't feel brave as I approached Veules les Roses. Once again, I had to control shaking arms and legs and a permanently aching stomach. But I wasn't going to let a little thing like that stop me.

I paused for a moment on the brow of the hill by the main road to make sure it was safe to carry on. Thankfully, there was no sign of the enemy, but I was shocked to see that now there were thousands and thousands of refugees. They blocked the road. Where would they all end up?

Then I looked towards the west. A huge cloud of black smoke filled the sky. At that moment, I realized that a choking smell had caught the back of my throat. What could it be?

I pushed my way across the road and sped into Veules les Roses. The main street was full of people, rushing about, looking nervously around. They were preparing to leave. Suddenly, I heard a roar overhead. I glanced up. German aircraft! I leapt off my bicycle and dodged into a doorway, my heart pounding. I didn't want to be shot at again. But they didn't fire and soon they were gone. I waited a while for my heart to slow down then I tore along the road and slipped into Hélène's little house.

I recited the message – that the German army is much too strong for our soldiers, the enemy have much bigger, better weapons, the British and French troops have had to withdraw and they've received orders to head for Le Havre where they'll be picked up by warships and taken to England.

Hélène gasped. "Not Le Havre!" she cried. She told me that the German army has already taken over the city. She asked me if I'd seen the black smoke in the west. I nodded. Then what she told me made me terrified for the soldiers who had gone that way. The smoke is from the oil refineries in the port. They've been bombed, destroyed by the German army and air force. She made me promise to tell Patrice to send word to the British and French soldiers. They must not go there. They'll run into a trap.

Her next piece of news was even worse. Apparently, General Rommel and the German army are surging this way from Le Havre. Our men and the British must head for

St Valery en Caux. Perhaps the ships will take them off from there. I repeated the message to check I had got it right.

When I delivered Hélène's message a short while later, Patrice looked shattered. He had deep worry lines across his forehead. Perhaps he was wondering who could take this message to the soldiers. It would be a very difficult and dangerous task. He glanced at me and opened his mouth to speak. Then he shut it again. He seemed undecided. Did he think I could do it? Then he thanked me and sent me home. I had to admit to myself as I left Patrice that I was secretly relieved I didn't have to go. The mission is too dangerous for a young girl, even a brave one!

Evening

Just now, I popped round to Yvette's. She seemed quiet. When I asked her if she was all right she nodded then shook her head. She was on the verge of tears as she admitted she's scared – of all that fighting in the village and the church and the German tanks and that bomb. It was so close she thought she was going to die.

She wanted to talk about everything and I was happy to listen. Suddenly, she became very agitated. Her eyes were fiery with anger as she told me she can't believe how much she hates the enemy. She said she'd do anything to get them out of our country. I stared at her. I've never seen my kind, gentle friend so mad. That got me thinking. Perhaps Yvette will be able to join our group after all! I'm going to ask Patrice.

When I got home, I came upstairs to write my diary, but a short while ago, I heard loud voices outside. A man was shouting, giving orders – in German! I shinned down the ladder and stepped outside. I saw a group of German soldiers near the level-crossing gates. I stared, frozen, unable to believe what I was witnessing. One by one the soldiers marched off along the railway line, just as the Scottish soldiers had done just a little while before. They were taking over the railway!

Mama stood in the doorway. She folded her arms and declared that she was *not* going to work for them. The German officer who had been giving orders marched over to me and Mama. He halted very stiffly, clicking his heels together and saluting. I took several steps back and stood close beside Mama. The officer began to speak. He spoke in French, but he had a very strong accent and he made lots of mistakes. Mama turned away from him. The officer told us he is in charge now. Mama didn't reply.

I watched the officer closely. At first, his face was calm. I think he was trying to be pleasant, but when Mama refused to speak or even turn back towards him his face began to twitch. Then he began giving orders. I winced at the harshness of his voice. Mama swung round towards him with a look of defiance on her face. She snapped at him – he may have won a small battle here, but the war is not over yet, not by a long way!

I held my breath, dreading his reaction. But at that moment, I heard a train coming. I looked along the railway. German soldiers had taken up their positions along the line. The train had reached the bend so the gates needed closing, but Mama did not move. The officer waited for a moment then he scowled at Mama and closed the gates himself.

The train trundled noisily through. It was full of German soldiers. I shuddered at the sight of them. Whatever Mama had said, the Germans had definitely taken charge. I heard the train stop at the station. Doors slammed. Men shouted. Soldiers swarmed everywhere. They think they own the place! This is *our* country.

The officer marched stiffly towards us and I clutched Mama's arm tightly. *Go away and leave us alone!* I shouted in my head. I desperately needed to yell it out loud, but I didn't want the German soldiers suspecting me of acting against them. I swallowed my anger and asked about the wounded soldiers in the village hall. He said they're prisoners of war and will be taken to camps in Germany. He had such a superior attitude. I wanted to go and punch him on the nose or scream in his ear, but I bit my lip and clenched my fists hard by my sides. I came back up here to write in my diary.

Monday 10th June
8 am

I'm so miserable. The page is blotchy with my tears. I hate the Germans with every part of me. I want to kick and punch and hit and bite and... Why? Because they're murderers, that's why!

I had a bad night. I was hot. I tossed and turned. I hated having those German soldiers outside and my brain was overflowing with questions again.

What's going to happen to us? Will they hurt us? Will the Scottish soldiers fall into the trap? Or will they escape?

I must have slept some of the time, but eventually, at first light, I decided to get up and go and see my hens. They always calm my nerves with their muttering and chattering and their heads on one side.

Quietly, I dressed and slipped down the ladder. I opened the back door and crept out into the garden, heading straight for the hen house. But as I came to the outer wire, I stopped. The door stood wide open. I ran to the doorway and stared in disbelief. I saw a few feathers lying among the uneaten grains of corn, but that was all that was left. My hands flew to my mouth and I smothered a scream. Then I sank on to my knees and I began to shudder with sobs.

My hens have gone!

10 am

When Mama came to find me, I had stopped crying, but was still huddled in the doorway of the hen house. I heard her gasp, and when I looked up I saw how pale she had become. Her mouth was clamped shut in a hard line, and I could tell she was almost as angry and upset as I was. "This isn't the work of the fox," she said.

There was a sound from the railway. A soldier was approaching. Mama stepped out and stood directly in his path. She went for him. She pointed towards the empty hen house and demanded to know how he dared to do this. The soldier held up his hand and shook his head. But Mama's eyes were flashing with anger as she demanded to speak with his officer. I couldn't bear to look at him; I was so full of disgust. He marched off towards the farm.

Mama put her arm round me – she knows how much I

loved my lovely hens. She almost made me cry again, but at that moment, we saw the officer marching towards us. Mama's anger burst out again and she yelled at him for ages, accusing him of all sorts of horrible crimes. The officer might not have understood every word, but he had understood the gist. His face was twitching again. I cringed. I didn't want Mama to get us into trouble. She told him he had no right to take the hens. He stepped menacingly towards us and shouted that he had every right now they're in charge.

That did it! I burst into tears again. Of course, we have always lived by our traditional French way of life and I accept it. The hens gave us eggs, but we would have eaten them eventually. That's how we live, here in the country, but not all at once. That's cold-blooded murder. The soldier bowed his head sharply and clicked his heels. Then he swivelled round and marched away.

I'll never get over it. I'm still crying now. I can't help it. It's not fair.

Midday

I've just been to Yvette's. It was creepy, cycling through the village, knowing that enemy soldiers had taken over, and I was glad I didn't see many of them, except a few standing on guard. But now I hate them with all my heart. I'll never forgive what they've done. I'll work harder from now on, to defeat them.

I was almost at her house when I saw something that made me wobble so violently that I nearly fell off my bicycle. Georges Dubois was talking to a German soldier! He was smiling, looking up at the soldier with admiration in his eyes. Georges is definitely a traitor to France. He's worse than the enemy! I wanted to spit, just like Grandma had done, but I gritted my teeth instead and managed to cycle on.

I told Yvette about my hens. She's very sympathetic. She says the soldiers are brutes! I came home the other way, to avoid having to see Georges again, but as I was passing the Cariat's house, Marcel came out of his front gate and I slowed down. There's a message to take. Marcel will be here shortly.

Sebastien came out to meet me when I reached home. He gave me a hug and muttered something about the hens. I stared at him, utterly amazed. Sebastien never hugs anyone, least of all me. It must be the war. It's turning us all into different people.

Thursday 13th June

I'm writing this now because I've been away from home and therefore I couldn't write in my diary. I might not get it all down in one go. Such a lot has happened over the past three days. I'll try and remember everything. Where have I been? Well, I'll begin where I left off, with Sebastien hugging me. I like to think about that. He's not such a bad brother, is he?

This is what happened on Monday afternoon

Half an hour after the "hug", I was on my way, carrying a letter for Hélène and a bag of home-made biscuits in my basket. I could hear distant sounds of gunfire as I pedalled along the lane. It was coming from the west. I wondered what was happening. Was it the Scottish regiment? Had they fallen into the German trap, as Hélène had warned? Or had Patrice managed to get a message to them? Perhaps even now, they were heading for St Valery en Caux to be rescued by ship.

As I rounded a bend, a column of German soldiers appeared, marching towards me. I gripped the handlebars hard and pedalled on. What should I do? If I stopped or turned round, they might be suspicious. So I decided to carry on, right past them. My heart pounded rapidly as I cycled by, but I needn't have worried. They kept their eyes firmly ahead and marched on. They didn't seem to notice me. I'm glad I look young for my age. None of them suspected a little French girl.

I crossed the main road safely, but I was just approaching Veules les Roses when I came across another group of German soldiers. They were all heavily armed and looked as if they were waiting for something. One of them held up his hand. This time I had to stop. I felt weak as I braked and jumped off my bicycle. My knees almost gave way as I stood shakily before him.

One of them asked where I was going and I answered, "To my aunt's house." I showed him the biscuits and said they were for her and my baby cousin. The soldier helped himself to a biscuit and took a bite. He nodded, finished the biscuit and passed the bag around. Soon all the biscuits were gone. One of the soldiers laughed and then they all joined in. I was seething. They had stolen my country and killed my hens. Now they were stealing everything else in sight and they thought it was funny! I don't know how I managed to control my temper this time, but I did. I bit my tongue and said nothing. I couldn't afford to annoy them.

Suddenly, the mood changed. I was told to empty my pockets. Slowly, I took my handkerchief, a piece of string and a pencil from my skirt pocket. The soldiers peered into the pocket, inspected my basket and stared at me with cold eyes, but they wouldn't find the note from Patrice to Hélène. As I left our village, I'd pushed it into my knickers, just in case!

Eventually, they waved me on, but I dared not relax until I was pedalling as innocently as I could away from them. I felt many pairs of eyes boring into my back as I went. At last, I gasped in air and tried to calm myself. It was getting really bad. The enemy was everywhere.

There was nobody on the street as I approached Hélène's house so I quickly left my bicycle in the usual place and knocked on the door. I slipped inside as soon as it was opened, but Hélène didn't even read the letter. She just snatched it from my hand, pushed me outside, told me to dash home and closed the door behind me. I was shocked by her hurry to get rid of me. Was the danger that close? Did she know something I didn't?

Suddenly, I heard the sound of gunfire. It didn't seem to be very far away. I wondered if the soldiers I had just met had received the orders they were waiting for. I dreaded that they might enter Veules les Roses at any minute. My legs were too shaky to ride my bicycle, but I was not going to leave it behind. The streets were still deserted as I pushed it up the hill towards Aunty Régine's house.

Keeping my head down and panting hard, I finally arrived at the house near the top of the cliff and ran round the back. Aunty Régine pulled me inside. She looked very scared and Charles was crying.

We went to the window. Across the little cove I could see the flashes of gunfire along the cliffs, from the port of St Valery en Caux. Then I stared out to sea. There was an oily black fog hanging over the water, but if I screwed up my eyes, I could just make out the shapes of quite a few large ships off the coast.

I thought they must have come to rescue the Scottish soldiers, but I didn't realize that I was thinking aloud until too late. I put my hand over my mouth. I'd let out a secret. Aunty Régine looked at me. She asked me how I knew that so I grinned and shrugged and tapped the side of my nose with my finger.

She's guessed I'm a... What am I? A spy?

I put my finger to my lips. I didn't want to lie to her, but I didn't deny anything either. It doesn't matter if she suspects what I'm up to. I trust her. She won't give my secret away.

This is what happened on Monday evening

The fighting seemed to be in and around St Valery en Caux, but I couldn't tell exactly where. If I stared really hard out of the window, I could see flashes of the guns along the cliffs.

I desperately wanted to get home. Mama would be out of her mind with worry. Several times I made up my mind to try, but each time I fetched my bicycle from behind the house, we imagined the fighting was coming nearer and I had to dash back inside. Aunty Régine wouldn't let me leave. She said it was much too dangerous. Maybe the Germans were fighting on the main road. My way would be blocked and I might be killed. That convinced me! I realized I'd have to wait there until it was safe to leave. Anyway, Sebastien knew where I was.

So I played with Charles for a while, but then I went to stand at the window. I found Uncle Thierry's binoculars and focused them along the coast. I became hypnotised! I had difficulty taking my eyes off the sight of the battle that was raging in the distance. It was like watching a film again, as if it wasn't really happening. I couldn't move away. Yet, just like in our village, I knew how real it was.

By supper time, I was still trapped. The battle at St Valery en Caux was really fierce. I heard massive explosions resounding along the coast. I saw German aircraft shoot overhead and dive-bomb the town. Off the coast, I noticed that the ships had come nearer to the shore. My brain was packed with questions I could not answer. Were they trying to evacuate our soldiers? Were the Scots fighting there? Was Angus still alive? Would he escape?

Was Uncle Thierry on one of those ships? I was sure Aunty Régine must be wondering the same thing, but she said nothing. After that first glimpse, she stayed away from the window. I don't think she could bear to look any longer.

Then the aircraft began to attack the warships, too, and I could see flashes from the anti-aircraft guns on the ships. All at once, I saw a great splash of water close to a ship. I gasped. The German tanks were firing out to sea. Several more shells landed near the ships. The ships returned fire. I couldn't believe it! The French ships were firing shells at their own land. I had a horrible thought – they might kill their own people.

Suddenly, through the binoculars, I picked out a smaller boat heading out to sea from the port of St Valery. It was full of people. It seemed to be making for one of the warships. But at that moment, a shell landed on the boat. It exploded in a ball of flames. I covered my eyes. They must all be dead, blown to pieces! I sat down, feeling sick.

After a few minutes, I couldn't resist looking again. More small boats were heading out to sea. Several reached the ships. Some soldiers were managing to escape!

By then, I thought I could see flames above St Valery en Caux. Huge plumes of smoke rose above the town. The fighting must be very fierce. How could the British and French soldiers defend it any longer? Would they surrender? Or would they, and all the people of St Valery, be killed?

This is what happened on Monday night

I stayed at Aunty Régine's window all evening. I didn't want to sleep although I ached all over, shattered by what I had witnessed along the coast. It was almost dark when Aunty Régine insisted. She more or less carried me to bed.

Even though I was exhausted, I was too restless to sleep well. I dozed a few times, but I kept snapping awake. I don't think Aunty Régine slept any more than I did. I could hear her walking about and I am sure I heard her crying.

The night was just as noisy as the day had been. The fighting raged on. I could hear gunfire and explosions. I got out of bed several times, but it seemed foggy and I couldn't see a thing except a glow from along the coast. Then I realized – the sounds were becoming louder. I found my way to my aunt's room and snuggled up to her. I felt safer there.

This is what happened on Tuesday 11th June

It gets harder and harder to write about these things. There are so many ghastly memories. But I want to write everything down as it happened if I can, so here goes.

As it began to grow light, I crept to the window. My eyes ached as I peered through the binoculars. Through the fog and drizzle, I could make out a ship that had come in close to the cliffs. The other ships were nearer than they had been the night before and some had come along into the little bay off Veules les Roses. Rowing boats and motor boats full of soldiers were trying to reach the ships. Some were succeeding, but German aircraft kept dive-bombing and there was heavy firing from the shore. Then I noticed things floating on the water, bobbing up and down on the waves. Bodies! I rushed away from the window and threw myself down on the bed, burying my head in the pillows. It was too horrible!

I couldn't eat any breakfast, not even when I saw Charles tucking in as usual. But after a while, I was drawn once again back to the window. Keeping my eyes off the sea below us,

I focused the binoculars along the cliffs. The fire was raging fiercely in St Valery en Caux and now I could see thousands of soldiers swarming along the cliffs.

Aunty Régine joined me at the window, with Charles held tightly in her arms. She had deep worry lines across her forehead. She said we were in terrible danger if we stayed where we were. But how could we leave? The fighting was moving in our direction. Soon the place would be swarming with soldiers and their weapons. Worst of all, I could see a giant tank creeping along the opposite cliff. We could be shot or blown to pieces. I wished we had left when I first arrived. It might have been safer then. Poor Aunty Régine! She felt so guilty. She said she would never forgive herself if anything happened to me. She would never be able to face my parents again.

I bit my lip to stop myself crying, thinking Mama and Papa must be worried out of their minds. Aunty Régine put her arm round me and we moved away from the window. I swallowed hard. I had to try and convince myself that the tanks wouldn't fire in our direction. It wasn't that easy. Charles began to whimper, so I found his cuddly blanket and gave it to him.

At that moment, without any warning, there was an enormous explosion, louder than I had ever heard before. The door crashed off its hinges and the window blew in. Glass splintered on to the floor. I think I screamed, but the next few moments were so confusing, I'm not sure what happened. I found myself cowering, with Aunty Régine and Charles, under the big oak table in the kitchen, absolutely petrified, too scared to cry.

We lay there on the floor for hours, with me gripping the table leg so hard my shoulders ached. I flinched at each explosion as the fighting went on and on outside. Aunty Régine's face was as pale as the cliffs below us. She just lay there, staring blindly at nothing. Charles was clinging to his mama and whimpering. Poor little boy! He didn't know what was going on. After a while, I started singing to him. It helped me cope with the noise and my fear. I began to feel a bit calmer. But all the while, I had one ghastly thought going round and round in my head. It only needed one of those shells to fly in our direction then it would be "Goodbye, Sophie". I didn't want to die.

The noise was deafening – the metallic rumbling of the tanks as they came nearer, the boom of the ships' guns, the whistle of the shells followed by the earth-shaking explosion as each one landed, the whining of the aircraft as they zipped overhead, the ack-ack-ack of their guns, the constant firing of machine guns, the sudden crack of rifles, the shouts and screams of men.

I wasn't thinking of the soldiers out there at that moment: how many were dying or wounded. All I could think of was: would we come out of this alive?

This is what happened on Wednesday 12th June, midday

The fighting carried on well into the night, but I must have gone to sleep eventually, even with all that noise. Suddenly, I was wide awake. I opened my eyes and listened. It was broad daylight though I've no idea what time it was. Everything had gone quiet. Aunty Régine and Charles were snuggled together, still fast asleep, so I slowly dragged myself out from under the table and stood up. I felt incredibly stiff in all my joints. Then I heard voices.

I hurried to the living room, treading carefully across the broken glass, and peered out of the window. I gasped. There were hundreds of soldiers quite close by. I couldn't tell which nationality most of them were, but I recognized the Germans that stood guard over them. (They wear dome-shaped helmets.) A few ships were still out there on the water, in the distance, except for one that seemed to be lying at a slight angle in the shallow water, pretty close to the beach. It was on fire.

I ran back to the kitchen and gently nudged Aunty Régine. She opened her eyes. For a moment, she didn't seem to realize where she was, then she blinked. I told her that the fighting had stopped. She said she guessed our soldiers must have surrendered. I couldn't help wondering: what's going to happen now? Are the Germans going to take over the whole of France?

It was time to escape. We grabbed all the food we could find and quickly collected together a few clothes and other essentials, bundled them up and headed out through the open doorway. I ran round the back of the house and found, to my relief, that my bicycle didn't seem to have been damaged. I pushed it round the front and loaded my basket with our things. Then we set off. Keeping our heads down, we ran down the road into the centre of the village. I don't know if the soldiers noticed us, but none of them called out and we weren't stopped.

My hand aches. I seem to have been writing for hours. More later.

This is what happened on Wednesday afternoon

The village of Veules les Roses was devastated. I was horrified at what we saw as we wove our way past deep holes in the road, burnt-out vehicles, weapons and piles of rubble that were the remains of some of the houses. I couldn't bear to look at the bodies lying there. There were so many! It was hideous!

We reached the Rue Victor Hugo. Suddenly, I stopped. I felt faint. I had to sit down on a low wall and put my head between my knees for a moment. I couldn't speak. I just pointed to a large mound of bricks where number 12 had been. Where was Hélène? A young lady appeared from behind the house next door, which was damaged but still standing. She must have seen us there. She told us what had happened. It was a direct hit. Hélène must have been killed instantly. I gasped and covered my mouth with my hands.

Aunty Régine was giving me a strange look. She asked if I had known Hélène. I nodded then shook my head. I wasn't supposed to let out these secrets, even to my own family. But it wouldn't matter so much now, would it? Now she was dead?

Then suddenly, I went cold all over. The thought still sends shivers cascading down my back. I'd been with her in that house. If Hélène had not sent me away ... that would have been the end of me! All I wanted was to get home.

The journey took us ages, because of the number of obstacles on the road and the number of other people like us who were escaping from their damaged or ruined homes. Anyway, I had no energy left and it was a struggle even to walk. But at last, we were there, on the edge of my village.

Suddenly, we were surrounded. Everyone was shouting

and crowding round us as if we were film stars. They were all thanking God that I was safe. They had thought I must be dead.

Someone must have run ahead of us. At that moment, Sebastien raced from the direction of our house. He flung himself at me, nearly knocking me over. It was the second hug I had had from him in a very short time, and if I hadn't been ready for tears again, I might have thought up something rude to say to him! But I felt too emotional for that, especially when I saw Mama and Papa not far behind him.

Mama shouted at me and asked me what I thought I was doing, going off like that! I could have got myself killed. She didn't realize how true that was! Then she burst into tears and flung her arms round me. Papa didn't say anything. He just gave me a giant squeeze and kissed the top of my head.

This is what happened late on Wednesday night

I felt quite depressed as we all made our way home. After the fear and excitement of the fighting and the shock of Hélène and all those bodies, I just wanted to bury my head somewhere and be left alone. I climbed the ladder and lay down on my bed, shutting out the sound of voices from downstairs. I didn't even have the energy to write in my diary.

After a while, I went downstairs. Mama was trying to arrange the furniture to fit a small bed in to a corner of the room. I'm going to sleep downstairs for a while so Aunty Régine and Charles can have my room. I don't mind. Why should I mind about something like that when there's a war going on only a few kilometres away? Mind you, I'll have to find a new hiding place for my diary.

Thursday 13th June 11 am
This is now today!

I slept fairly well in my new "bedroom". Early this morning, I heard someone calling me. Then Yvette came in. I felt better for seeing her. I even managed to joke that I didn't need a nurse! Then I told her what had happened. She asked me why I had been to Veules les Roses – I must have known it would be dangerous. I lied that I wanted to see my aunt. She laughed. You can't fool Yvette – not when you've been her best friend all your life. She knows there's another reason. And I haven't had a chance to ask Patrice yet.

I admitted that I was doing something else, but I still

93

couldn't tell her what. I almost did. I wanted to share my feelings about Hélène. I've promised her that I'll talk to someone first and that if he agrees, I'll tell her.

I walked into the village with Yvette. I left her at her house and hurried to Patrice's place. I ran quickly up the path and round the back. I knocked on the kitchen door and it was immediately opened. Patrice looked so relieved to see me. He apologized. He's been feeling bad about sending me with that message. He doesn't know how the news got round that I had gone to Veules les Roses, but the whole village has been talking about me.

I told him the sad news about Hélène. It was really odd. Perhaps war has made some people hard and unfeeling, but when he asked me how she died and I told him about the house being flattened and that she would have died instantly and not suffered, I couldn't believe his reaction. He was just glad that she hadn't been able to give away any secrets! Nothing else. Sometimes I just don't understand how other people's minds work.

Then I told him about Yvette. I said I was sure she would be trustworthy, and he's promised to think about it. I'm not convinced he's really going to think very hard about her because he changed the subject immediately. He says we need a new contact in Veules les Roses.

I called in on Grandma on the way home and told her all about my adventure in Veules les Roses.

6 pm

I've found a new hidey-hole for this diary. It's not as convenient as my own room, of course, but I think it's a very good place – under the nesting boxes in the hen house!

Also, for the first time in ages I've got something happy to write in my diary. Well, I hope it's happy because I'm extremely worried as well. I'll write about how my good news happened.

There's still no school. I've been feeling really restless and I can't settle down to anything. My brain is so full of everything that happened in Veules les Roses so I cycled over to Yvette's this afternoon. She's itching to hear Patrice's answer.

I told her I had other things on my mind. I needed to find out what was going on. What's happened to all those soldiers? Did their leaders surrender? Are they all prisoners? I suggested to her that we could go up to the main road and see if there's anything happening. She was scared that it would be dangerous. I told her we'd be fine because the fighting had stopped, although I was a bit apprehensive, too.

As we sped along the lane, I told her about when I had first seen the refugees. I thought we could go to the same spot because we would get the best view from there.

Before we reached the brow of the hill, we could hear the rhythmic crunch of marching feet. Then we saw them. A long column of soldiers stretched in both directions as far as we could see; thousands and thousands of them, French, English and Scottish, I guessed, marching away from Veules les Roses. They were all prisoners of war.

German guards marched on both sides of the road. From the way the prisoners were moving, I thought they looked dejected and tired. Lots of them were bandaged, many were limping and some were being carried on stretchers. I felt so sorry for them. They must feel miserable. How far would they have to walk? Where would they end up? Was Angus among them?

Suddenly, a familiar sound carried up towards us and an enormous smile spread over my face. It was the weird howl and groan of the bagpipe. It was the Scottish soldiers. We could see the piper striding proudly along in his kilt. At least he was still alive! Quite near the piper, I noticed a soldier with a massive bandage round his head. He was limping badly. At that moment, the soldier fell down. Yvette must have been watching him, too, because we both gasped.

Then the soldier neatly rolled over and dropped into the ditch at the side of the road. None of the German guards had noticed! I couldn't be sure whether he was so badly wounded that he couldn't go on or whether he had done it on purpose. Was he trying to escape?

But there was no way we could find out. We couldn't go down there to investigate. We just had to wait. The crocodile of prisoners kept coming and coming and I couldn't believe how many there were, but at last they had all gone. The road was empty.

I was expecting the soldier to climb out of the ditch, but nothing happened. I looked at Yvette and I'm sure she was thinking exactly the same thing. Perhaps he was really badly wounded. Perhaps he hadn't rolled over on purpose. Perhaps he needed our help.

Keeping an eye out for any remaining German soldiers, we crept down the slope towards the road. As we approached the ditch, I thought I heard a sound and I dodged down, pulling Yvette down with me. We waited and listened. There it was again – a low moaning noise. Yvette's eyes lit up with excitement. We both knew it was the soldier.

I crept slowly forward, feeling tense, ready to spring back and run for it. I don't know why, but I was half expecting him to leap up like a Jack-in-a-box at any moment. But we reached the ditch and peered down into it. There, at the bottom, lying in a few centimetres of water, was the soldier. The bandage round his head was dirty and covered in splashes of blood. He was groaning and his muddy face was twisted in pain. But I instantly noticed the brilliant blue eyes that were staring up at us. There was something familiar about those eyes.

Suddenly, I gasped. Angus? I jumped down into the ditch. I showered questions on him, which I'm sure he didn't understand. What had happened to him? Was he badly hurt? Where were they being taken? Were the German soldiers good to them? I wiped some of the mud from his face and could see how deathly pale he was underneath. He must have lost a lot of blood. He was shivering, too, so I thought he might have a fever. He looked very ill and I felt his forehead. It was hot. Then I glanced up at Yvette, who was staring down with a look of disbelief on her face.

She wanted to know how I knew his name, but I said I'd tell her later. Angus needed a doctor, but when I suggested that to him, he certainly understood and I saw fear in his eyes. He tried to get up. He made me promise that I wouldn't fetch a doctor. I guessed he couldn't trust anyone. A doctor might give him away. He's an escaped prisoner of war. If he's caught now, he'll be shot. But if I didn't fetch a doctor, was Angus going to die? I tried to lift him, but I couldn't budge him. He seemed to be stuck in the mud at the bottom of the ditch.

After heaving and pushing for ages, I helped him shift to one side, so he wasn't lying in the water, then climbed back up to Yvette. I'd had an idea. I leaned over the ditch and told Angus to stay where he was (as if he could do anything else) and said we'd be back as soon as we could.

I'm at the house now. Yvette went home, but she's coming

back soon, and I've sneaked down the garden. I'm trying to ignore the German guard at the level crossing and I'm sitting on the hens' feeding trough writing this! I've been trying to organize some help, but it's been difficult and now I'm waiting for Sebastien to get the next part sorted out. I'm feeling so impatient. We need to get back to Angus as quickly as we can. I couldn't bear it if he died. It has done me good to write it all down.

Evening

Phew! What a hectic, terrifying, exciting time we've had!

On the way home, I had told Yvette how I knew Angus and revealed my idea for his rescue, which ended with him hiding up in our house. I was sure we could make it work, but when I told Mama, she went into a panic and told me we'd all get shot. Also she reminded me that we didn't have any room now Aunty Régine and Charles are here.

Anyway, we soon got round that. Grandma came into the kitchen. She had overheard our conversation and offered to look after Angus herself. She repeated that it would take more than a few Germans to finish her off! In the end, it was Aunty Régine who came up with the answer.

She is going to stay at Grandma's with Charles so that leaves room for Angus.

At that moment, Sebastien arrived home with Marcel and Olivier. I looked at Grandma and put my finger to my lips. Of course, we knew we could trust Marcel and Sebastien, but Olivier wasn't in our group. You can never be sure! I took Sebastien out into the garden to explain what Yvette and I had been doing. He was really impressed with me. He beckoned to Marcel and they had a private conversation. A few minutes later, Olivier went home to the farm.

That was when I went to the hen house to write about everything. Then Yvette came back and we stood by the front gate, waiting. Sebastien and Marcel were nowhere to be seen. We had to get back to Angus. Suppose the Germans found him before we got back. Suppose he died before we could save him. My life seemed to me to be one waiting game after another.

But I was totally amazed ten minutes later, when Olivier Masson crossed over the railway line and stopped outside our gate. He was sitting high up on his papa's cart, which was being drawn by an old bay mare. On the back of the cart was a large pile of straw. Sebastien was running behind the cart. Olivier grinned. He's one of us and I didn't even realize it.

Yvette and I scrambled up on to the cart behind Olivier. Sebastien rode up front. It was a very bumpy ride and Yvette and I had to hang on tightly, but I didn't care. It had been my idea, to borrow Mr Masson's cart, but I had been wondering how I could explain it to Mr Masson without giving anything away. It had been easier than I thought. I was really pleased that Olivier was one of us! As we rode we concocted a story about where we were going and what we were doing, in case we were questioned.

We reached the brow of the hill overlooking the main road and Olivier stopped the cart. We all glanced around us. After all the activity of the past few days, it was uncannily quiet. I slipped down and ran to the ditch while Oliver took the cart down on to the main road. I knelt at the side of the ditch and peered down. I told Angus we'd come to rescue him.

His eyes were closed and my heart lurched. Was he dead? To my relief, his eyes fluttered open and he tried to smile, then he winced. He was obviously in dreadful pain, but at least he was alive! I beckoned to the others. I'm glad we had the two boys with us. They may not be equal to us girls in many ways, but I have to admit their superior strength was very useful!

Gently, Sebastien and Olivier pushed a wide plank of wood underneath Angus. He cried out as they moved him. Yvette and I kept a look-out. Then the boys carefully raised him out of the ditch and on to the cart. We covered him in straw then quickly climbed up ourselves. Olivier flicked the reins and clicked out of the side of his mouth to set the horse in motion. The whole operation had only taken us about five minutes.

The journey back to the village seemed to last forever. No one spoke. We were all feeling too tense. My brain was racing. Supposing we met a German patrol? Would our made-up story convince them? Would they search the cart and find Angus?

We had almost reached the village when I heard the sound of a motorbike heading our way. As it came towards us I could see the dome-shaped helmet I recognized so well. I felt disgust in the pit of my stomach. A German!

I whispered to Angus to keep still and stay quiet. I just hoped he understood me. I crossed my fingers and everything else I could think of and held my breath as the German approached. Would he speed right by? Then my worst nightmare was happening. He was slowing down.

As he came alongside the cart, he stopped. He held up his hand and Olivier pulled on the reins. The horse obeyed and the cart came to a standstill. I prayed that Angus would not give us away. The German sat astride his motorbike, keeping the engine running, and indicated with a wave that we should all get down. He spoke quite good French. He asked where we were going. Olivier said we were going home to the farm. He looked the German in the eye, but I could hear a slight tremor in his voice. The German nodded. He pointed at the straw and asked what it was.

I put on my best appealing expression as I told him it was straw for the animals, but I desperately hoped he wouldn't notice my entire body shaking.

The German frowned and said that it's summer so the animals are in the fields and don't need straw. Luckily, we had thought of this! Olivier was ready with the answer: that he has two sick horses that need fresh straw every day.

I couldn't make out whether the German had understood, but his frown didn't go away. He pointed at the straw, which was piled in an untidy heap on the cart. Then he formed a bundle with his hands. I almost panicked. We hadn't anticipated this question. Why wasn't the straw in a bundle? I dare not look at the others in case we gave ourselves away. I had to think fast. Suddenly, I had a brainwave.

I smiled and lowered my eyes. Then I tried to look highly embarrassed, pointed at Olivier and said that he was my boyfriend. Yvette caught on. She pointed at Sebastien and told the German that they were in love. I don't know how she managed it, but she actually blushed! Both the boys looked stunned for a second then they nudged each other and grinned sheepishly at the soldier.

The German looked from one to another of us. I could see the cogs of his brain working it all out. Two boys, two girls, the girls' clothes covered in bits of straw, one of the girls blushing, the other one seeming shy, the boys looking pleased with themselves… He was coming to the conclusion I had hoped for – that we had all been rolling in the straw!

After a moment, a slow smile replaced the frown on the German's face. The engine roared and he accelerated away. We stood there for ages, unable to move. It was Olivier who broke the silence. He patted the top of my head and said he didn't know I cared! I grinned, the relief flooding into me now the immediate danger was over. Then I noticed Sebastien staring at Yvette as if he was seeing her for the first time. She was still blushing. Maybe it hadn't all been an act! Is she really in love with my brother? Is he in love with her, too? I'm totally amazed!

We climbed back on to the cart and trundled into the village. When Olivier halted the cart close to our gateway, I jumped down, crept to the corner of the house and peered along the railway. There were two German soldiers about 25 metres away. They were smoking and talking and not looking in our direction. Luckily, there was no one on guard at the crossing gates. I kept watch while Olivier and Sebastien carefully lifted the wooden stretcher down. It took less than a minute to carry Angus inside.

Just as the German soldier returned to his post at the gates, Olivier leapt back on to the cart and flicked the reins. The horse began to walk and Olivier drove the cart across the track, waving to the soldier as he went. Yvette and I hurried indoors. Angus was lying on my bed in the corner and Mama was bending over him. She looked worried. Then she looked up and her eyes were angry. "We'll show those German soldiers," she whispered.

Late

We're waiting for the doctor to come.

A little while ago, Angus stirred in his sleep, but he didn't wake up. He looked dreadful. I wanted to start cleaning him up straight away, but Mama thought we should get him upstairs first. My room is empty because Aunty Régine and Charles have already gone to Grandma's. Sebastien argued that Angus is too ill to move and, anyway, too heavy to lift up the ladder.

Yvette felt Angus's pulse. Seeing her do that made me feel incredibly jealous of her. He's *my* soldier. I'm the one who befriended him at the crossing barrier. I'm the one who recognized him in the ditch. I'm the one who thought up the plan for his rescue. I don't want Yvette taking over! I'm the one to care for Angus.

So I persuaded Mama to fill a bowl with warm water mixed with disinfectant. She found an old sheet and ripped it into strips then she dipped a strip into the water. I took it from her and squeezed the liquid from the cloth, gently wiping more dirt and dried blood from Angus's face. Then I took some little scissors and began to cut at the bandage. I had to grit my teeth. I dreaded what I might find underneath. As I unwound the lengths of cloth, I revealed his tangled hair, matted with sweat, mud and blood. Then I saw the wound.

I gasped and turned my eyes away, feeling dizzy. The gash is deep and long. It stretches from his forehead right across the crown of his head, like a parting drawn by a deadly comb. I wonder how it had happened. If it had been two centimetres lower, he would have been killed!

When I made myself look back, I found Angus's eyes on me. He began mumbling and muttering, but I didn't understand what he was trying to say. So I began to bathe the wound as gently as I could. He was so brave. He winced a few times, but didn't cry out although it must have been dreadfully painful. Yvette was watching closely.

The more I washed the wound, the more I realized how deep it is. He needs stitches. All around the cut, Angus's head is red and looks very sore. It must be infected. That must be why he has a fever. Even Yvette, who was such a good nurse to the other Scottish soldiers, hasn't the skill to heal this or to bring his temperature down.

Sebastien ran round to Patrice Cariat's house. He is sure there must be a doctor in the network. I carried on washing away all the dirt in the wound and Mama fetched several changes of water. Angus began tossing and turning on the little bed. He was awake one minute and in a deep sleep the next. He seemed to be getting worse. Sometimes, he groaned and his face was screwed up in pain. His head felt so hot. I was really worried. I knew he desperately needed the doctor. I wished Sebastien wasn't taking so long.

Papa came home from working late at the farm a few minutes ago. He wanted to know what on earth we were doing, getting ourselves in danger for the sake of this young Scotsman, but I'm sure he didn't mean anything. He soon recovered from the shock of seeing Angus and he's on our side, of course.

We were all going mad with impatience by the time Sebastien came back. (He smiled at Yvette. She blushed again. Yuck! Fancy being in love with my brother!) Then he told us about a doctor in Luneray who can be trusted. Patrice has gone to fetch him now. Sebastien has a coded message to say when he arrives. The doctor has to reply then we'll know it's really him.

I feel that same shiver of excitement as when I took that first message to poor Hélène. We're really involved – the fighting, the enemy outside, an escaped prisoner and now another coded message. Then I look down at the pale thin face and my worry returns. I wish the doctor would hurry up and come.

Very late

At last, he's been.

I heard the noise of a bicycle being leant against the wall outside. I held my breath, praying it was the doctor, not an enemy soldier. There was a sharp knock on the door and I felt my stomach tighten. We all looked at each other in silence as Sebastien went to the door. I heard him speak, "It'll be a full moon tonight." I held my breath, waiting for the reply. A deep voice replied, "But there are storms heading our way." Was it the right answer?

It must have been, because Sebastien let him in. I let out a loud sigh. Yvette did the same. She was obviously feeling as tense as I was. The doctor said his name is Dr Boulais. He's quite young with dark hair and deep brown eyes. He went straight over to Angus and felt his pulse. Then he peered closely at the wound. Angus opened his eyes. He tried to sit up and push the doctor away, but I told him it was all right and that this doctor is a friend.

Angus relaxed back on to the bed and closed his eyes again. Dr Boulais washed his hands then began working on the wound. He said I'd done a good job of cleaning it up.

His praise made me feel warm inside. I smiled at him and stayed close by as he found a needle and thread in his bag and began to stitch. Yvette watched closely, but Sebastien went up to his room. He's a bit squeamish.

The doctor was almost finished when there was another knock at the door. Everyone froze. We all stared at each other with wide eyes, not daring to move or make a sound. Who could it be? Mama went to the door. I heard her open it. Then I heard her talking and another female voice answering. It was only Yvette's mama. What a relief!

Yvette headed for the door. She said she'd better go home with her mama now and she'd see us tomorrow. I said something to her that I regret. I warned her not to tell her mama about Angus. She glared at me as if she would like to see me taken away by the enemy. Of course she won't, any more than I will and I know I'd be offended if anyone said that to me, but I couldn't help saying it. I've upset her. I hope she'll forgive me.

When the doctor had finished, he said how dangerous it is here with the German guards outside. He didn't need to remind us that one of the soldiers could glance through the window and see Angus. He thought we should try and get him upstairs. So Sebastien and Papa pulled from above and Dr Boulais pushed from below and they managed to lift Angus up the ladder. Now he's sleeping peacefully in my bed.

Dr Boulais is very worried about Angus. He's coming back tomorrow. I hope Angus won't die in the night – especially in my bed.

Friday 14th June

He didn't die in the night, but he's still desperately ill. I've spent all day sitting beside him. I've bathed his forehead and given him sips of water. He's slept most of the time, so I've been reading my English book and practising some phrases.

Dr Boulais came this morning. He told us he left his bicycle behind a hedge and came across the fields to our house. He wants to avoid being stopped by the German guards. He thinks Angus will pull through, as he puts it. I hope that means he's going to get better.

Mama says she heard on the wireless that many people have fled from Paris because they fear the Germans are going to attack.

Evening

About seven o'clock this evening, I heard a tap on the door. I crept to the top of the ladder and listened as Mama opened it. I'm sure my heart stopped beating for a moment and I almost overbalanced and fell headfirst down the ladder when I heard who it was – Georges Dubois! What did he want? Not me, for certain. I know well what he thinks of me! So I thought it must be about Angus, but it couldn't be. No one knows about him, except for my family, plus Olivier, Marcel, Patrice, Dr Boulais and Yvette. And they wouldn't give him away, would they?

Mama asked him what he wanted and he asked if Sebastien was in. Mama said he was over at the farm. I was dying to warn Mama about Georges, but I had to stay silent and still and I just hoped she wouldn't invite him in. Luckily, Georges just said it didn't matter and it wasn't important, then he left.

Mama closed the door and came to the bottom of the ladder. She looked worried. She told me that there's something about Georges that she can't quite put her finger on and I said I knew what it was. Then I told her that he likes the Germans being here! And I added that he knows what I think.

That scares me. And I don't reckon he came to see Sebastien at all. It was just an excuse to come here, I'm sure. We're going to have to be extra careful from now on, if he's going to be snooping around.

Saturday 15th June

Today we heard some terrible news on the wireless. The Germans have taken over Paris:

"There has been fighting in the streets. German swastika flags are flying from all the important buildings. Thousands of people are streaming out of the city, some in cars, but most of them on foot. They are fleeing in every direction. As they escape, many of these refugees are being attacked from the air. Enemy planes have dive-bombed or cut through the crowds with machine-gun fire. Hundreds are being killed or wounded."

I shuddered, remembering the way those aircraft had attacked me. Those German airmen are cowards. Our capital city is in the hands of the enemy. What will happen now?

Evening

Angus is still sleeping most of the time. He tosses and turns, and I've been sitting with him, bathing his head with cold water to try to lower his temperature. I don't feel jealous of Yvette now. She's been round and I let her spend some time by his bedside. She seems to have forgiven me for what I said. She was bursting with excitement when she arrived. Patrice has allowed her to join the group. Well, he couldn't really refuse after she helped rescue Angus, could he? I gave her a big hug. I'm really pleased, too. It's like old times. I don't have to keep secrets from my best friend now.

Dr Boulais came again. He thinks there is some sign of improvement, and Angus's temperature is down so the cold water must be doing some good. When the bandages were changed, I could see that the wound isn't so infected. It's healing well.

Sunday 16th June

Angus is definitely improving. Today, I managed to persuade him to drink some soup. He opens his eyes quite often. They're so blue. He smiles a lot, too, and keeps thanking me. Dr Boulais says he's so pleased with Angus that he won't come tomorrow unless we call him. He'll come back the next day to take out the stitches.

This evening, after the doctor had gone, Georges came round again. Sebastien saw him cycling down the lane and went out to meet him. I watched from the window. They talked for a few minutes then Georges went away. When Sebastien came inside he was seething. He called Georges a German-loving moron. Neither of us can stand him. I asked Sebastien what Georges wanted. He apparently asked to borrow a bicycle pump. I couldn't believe it. What a feeble excuse!

We understand his game. We're sure he doesn't know about Angus or we would have had a visit from the enemy by now, but he suspects we're up to something. He also asked Sebastien why he is suddenly much friendlier with Marcel than he used to be. We know Georges is dangerous.

We'll have to be even more careful and warn the others. He just needs to pick up one piece of evidence and we'll have real problems.

Monday 17th June

Shocking news! We all listened to the wireless this evening. Our Prime Minister is a traitor. He's asked the Nazis (these are the real nasty Germans who are true followers of Hitler) for an armistice (a kind of peace treaty) where our leaders would sign an agreement that says we don't mind the Germans taking over France. What a lie! Of course we mind – very much. This is terrible. We're all devastated. I'm also extremely angry.

Angus is getting stronger. If I help him to sit up he manages to eat a bit.

Evening

The postman came today, which is really surprising considering what's been going on. He had a letter for me. I felt so excited as I took the envelope. I had recognized the writing. It's from Anais. I quickly ripped it open and pulled out a single sheet of paper. I could hardly read it through my tears:

Dear Sophie,

I hope this reaches you without any trouble. After we left your lovely village we walked for several more days. We had to hide from the German army three times along the route, but eventually we came to the River Seine. We had difficulty getting across. We were stopped by German sentries on the bridge and I thought they were going to take Mama prisoner because she had lost one of her papers.

Then we walked and walked and walked. I thought we would never stop. At last we were picked up by a very kind farmer and he took us to his farmhouse. We are settled well here, but we have to work from sunrise to sunset as all the men have gone to war. It is hard, but at least we have a roof over our heads and we are not hungry.

I hope the war does not reach you. Please write if you can and tell me how you and your family are doing. You can reach me at the farm (the address is at the top of the letter).

We still have no news of my Papa, but we still pray all the time.

Grosses bises,

Anaïs

I'm so relieved she's found somewhere safe, but it must be so sad not knowing where your papa is or whether he is alive or dead. I've decided to write back to her. Mama's warned me not to tell her any details about what's been happening here. She said my letter could fall into enemy hands. I shall be very careful. After the cruelty I've seen lately, I don't want to risk anything.

Tuesday 18th June

Yesterday, our most important military leader, General de Gaulle, fled to England. He's spoken out against our government and so he's an enemy to them as well as the Germans. He's going to live over there, in exile. Some people are calling him a coward, running away from France when we're in trouble, but Papa thinks it's the best place for him to be to try and help the French people. If he stayed in France he could be captured and imprisoned or executed and then he wouldn't be any help to our country.

We managed to pick up a wireless broadcast from London. This is what General de Gaulle said:

"Frenchmen, Frenchwomen. Be strong. Keep fighting. The War will be won. Whatever happens, the flame of French Resistance must not and will not be extinguished."

That's exactly what we believe in! It makes me even more determined to go on fighting.

Angus had his stitches out today. He looked very pale and winced a lot as Dr Boulais pulled them out one by one. I feel proud of myself. I didn't mind watching – not like Sebastien. I thought he was going to faint.

Wednesday 19th June

I'm all of a flutter. It's Angus. I think I'm in love with him! This evening, I was sitting beside him, reading my English book as the light began to fade. Suddenly, he whispered my name. It made me jump and I felt a blush spread over my face.

I spoke to him in English and asked how he was feeling. He told me he's much better. He smiled. He's really good-looking when he does that! And his eyes – they're so brilliant blue and sparkly. Then he started talking much too quickly. I held up my hand to stop him. From then on we spoke half English, half French. We coped quite well.

He asked me where he was and how he got here. Of course, I told him about Sebastien, Yvette and Olivier and the ditch and the cart and even the German motorcyclist. He listened in silence then he thanked me. We're gradually beginning to understand each other more and more. He's sitting up most of the time now although he sometimes feels dizzy.

Mama came upstairs with some food for him. She says he needs to build up his strength. He smiled at Mama and thanked her for everything. He knows he's putting us all in danger and that he can't stay here much longer. I don't want him to go. I told him he's too ill to be moved.

The door opened downstairs. It was Sebastien. He had been at the Cariats' house all evening. He came up the ladder. Apparently, Patrice says we must move Angus as soon as possible. He knows a safe house where Angus can stay until he is strong enough to travel. I wanted to argue that he's safe here, but I know that's not true, especially since Sebastien told us some bad news. He's worried about the guards outside, but worse than that, Georges and a couple of his friends have been asking more questions. Even worse than that, Sebastien is sure he was followed this evening.

I bit my lip. I was too full of emotion to speak. I have to admit it really is becoming too dangerous to keep Angus in our house. What would happen to all of us if he was discovered? Anyway, there's a plan. We just have to hope no one finds him before tomorrow. Tomorrow, after dark, Angus will leave.

I've just closed the shutters. A guard was watching me from his post at the barrier. I instantly froze inside, but I tried to act normally. Does he suspect anything? Is he about to come knocking on our door and arrest us all?

Thursday 20th June

This morning, Sebastien brought Angus a bundle of his clothes and told him to put them on. Angus nodded. Sebastien told him to try and practise walking, but to stay out of sight of the windows. He also said that Marcel will be coming round this afternoon with instructions. I'll have several jobs to do. Then we all have to be ready when the signal comes.

I've felt twitchy all morning, listening for the guard outside, dreading the sharp rap on the door and thinking of what we had to do later on. I came downstairs so that Angus could get changed in private. I could hear him moving about in my room above. His footsteps sounded unsteady and slow. Later, I climbed the ladder and went to join him. Angus was sitting on the bed, dressed in Sebastien's clothes. He looked so different. Really French! I giggled, but then I saw he had such a sad expression on his face. He told me he kept having flashbacks of the battle in St Valery en Caux. Many of his friends died, he told me.

He seemed to want to talk about it so I sat down beside him. Half in English, half in French, he told me all about it. He began with the strong German attack as his regiment tried to defend the port. I understood some of what he said and guessed a lot more. Some of it I knew already. The soldiers had been ordered to fight as long as possible to protect St Valery, then there was the promise of warships coming to rescue them. They fought like dogs, but there were German tanks and planes. The Scottish and French soldiers only had their smaller weapons.

They had to go down into the town, which was on fire by then. (I knew about this – I saw it from Aunty Régine's window.) He saw people running in terror. Then after hours of fighting, the French General surrendered. Angus was shocked. Scotsmen don't like to give in. They always fight to the end. So they fought on. His best friend, Jock, was killed right in the centre of St Valery en Caux.

Angus had tears in his eyes. I felt choked, too, so I held his hand and we sat in silence for a while. Then he was ready to go on. He remembered rain and black fog over the sea. He saw that the ships had arrived so they went to the port, but the enemy aircraft were dive-bombing and they couldn't leave. So they went along the cliffs. It was then that something hit his head. Next thing he knew, his head was bandaged and he discovered that they had surrendered. Straight away, he knew he had to escape.

He lay down and turned his face to the wall. I guess it was all too much for him, telling me about something so dreadful that had happened to him such a short time ago. I left him for a while, and when I returned with some hot chocolate and some warm bread from the baker, he rolled over and looked up at me.

I'm blushing as I write this! He told me how kind I am and that he likes me. The blood rushed to my face and there was an ache in my chest. It was so different from the feelings I had for Georges. How can I have imagined that I was in love with him? It's Angus I'm in love with! I kissed his cheek and he blushed, too. Is he in love with me?

He took my hand and reminded me (as if I wanted to be reminded) that he has to leave tonight. I nodded. I didn't dare speak for fear of bursting into tears.

Later

Marcel came around lunchtime with the plans for Angus's escape. By the time he had finished, I realized I had an important part to play. I've been extremely busy this afternoon. I've had a list of jobs to do and an enormous amount to memorize. I was itching to begin, even though I knew that this meant Angus would be leaving us. Just before Marcel left, he gave me a coded message and two written ones. He told me not to let anyone get their hands on these messages. He warned me that it's not only the German soldiers we have to watch, but there are several French people like Georges who are befriending the enemy. They wouldn't hesitate to betray us.

I promised him that the messages would be safe. I'll hide them in my knickers – not that I'd tell him that!

So off I went, always remembering Marcel's warning to be careful. First, I called at a house in Luneray and delivered the coded message. I said, "The wheat is ready to be harvested," to the young woman who opened the door. I waited nervously for her answer. She smiled then replied, "And everyone is ready to harvest it." It was the right answer.

Then I told her the full message. I was pleased that my first job had gone well.

Next I cycled to a little village a few kilometres away. As I entered the village, I had a creeping sensation on the back of my neck. I was convinced I was being followed, but every time I looked round, there was no one there. Just to be sure, I dodged round a few corners and doubled back. I'm pretty quick on my bicycle and I must have shaken off my follower, if there was one.

I felt very tense all the while as I left the two written messages, one under a flowerpot and the other behind a loose brick in a wall. I didn't relax until I was safely home again.

Papa was working over at the farm as usual and Sebastien was not at home. It seemed very quiet in the house. I could tell Mama was not in a good mood. All her movements were hurried and jerky. She snapped at me when I got in her way. She's had a letter from her bosses ordering her to obey the Germans. She's livid, but if she refuses she'll lose her job – apart from making the soldiers angry – and she doesn't want that.

Angus was in the living room, walking slowly around, but keeping well away from the window, as instructed. He kept clutching his hands together and frowning and taking deep breaths. I stayed there with him. I think he feels the same as me. He doesn't really want to leave, but at the same time, he can't wait for it all to be over.

Late

He's gone! I'm heartbroken!

It was quite dark. We were waiting for Sebastien, Marcel and Olivier to arrive and the escape plan would begin. Mama had just come in from opening the crossing gates for the final train of the day when we heard voices outside. It didn't sound like any of the boys or Papa. It must have been instinct, but I had this horrible feeing that we were in deadly danger.

I hissed at Angus and beckoned for him to follow me. I dashed to the back window, opened it, checked that there was no one around and jumped out. I had to help Angus climb over the sill then, keeping low, we ran through the garden to the empty hen house. I opened the door and shoved him in, pushing him down behind the nesting boxes, close to where I hide this diary.

There was no time to pause there. As I dashed back to the house and climbed back in through the window, I could hear raised voices in the kitchen. Mama was shouting, "How dare you?" It was Georges Dubois she was shouting at. It seemed he had walked into the house uninvited. Mama told him Sebastien wasn't at home, but he said they hadn't come to see Sebastien. They had come to see what he called "our visitor".

I stayed where I was, listening. There was someone else in the kitchen. Who was with Georges? Then I heard a second voice. He was speaking French, but with a strong accent – a German accent! He said he believed we had a guest staying here. Mama's so good at thinking on her feet. She laughed and pretended she thought they meant Aunty Régine and little Charles. She rattled on about how their house in Veules les Roses was badly damaged by the German attack.

But the German interrupted. He said it was not Mama's sister or her infant they wanted to see, but a male. I stepped into the kitchen at that moment. I went up to Georges and smiled at him although my guts were churning uncontrollably. I mentioned Sebastien, but Georges snapped back. He said he already knew he's not here. So I quizzed him. So why was he here? Then I put on my very best act (while feeling sick). I stepped closer and asked him if the truth was that he's in love with *me*!

Mama and the German looked astonished, but the expression on Georges's face was grotesque. It was so ugly. He stepped back from me and told me angrily not to be so ridiculous. I don't know where this would have led if Sebastien had not arrived at that moment with Olivier and Marcel. Georges went for them, saying he knew we had someone staying here. I have to admire my coolness, even though everyone must have noticed my shaking limbs. I told him the truth – that there was no one in this house except us, and that if he would like to search, that was fine by everyone here.

I saw a startled look in Marcel's eyes, but Sebastien and Olivier have seen my acting before. They didn't look too worried.

Georges and the soldier searched the whole house. Georges seemed confident at first, talking loudly and laughing. He was so certain of himself, but gradually he grew quieter and then silent. A frown developed across his forehead and I could see he was becoming angry. He had been so sure he was right.

I was beginning to feel confident that Angus was safe, but suddenly, Georges reached the living-room window. He stood still and grimaced at me. Then he began laughing loudly as he pointed through the darkness. He was convinced that he knew where our visitor was – "in Sophie's precious hen house!"

He shot out of the back door, turned on a powerful torch and raced across the grass with all of us close behind him. I felt sick and so scared I could hardly force my legs to carry me, but when Georges rushed through the enclosure and burst into the little wooden building, I thought I would die of relief. It was empty!

Georges was furious. He shouted at us all – we had

won this time, but he knows there's something going on and he'll get us next time. He stormed back up the garden with the German soldier on his tail, leaving us quaking and quivering in the darkness. I burst into tears. I had no idea where Angus was.

Suddenly, Angus emerged out of the darkness and came and stood close to me. Luckily, he had guessed his hideout might be found. I hugged him, but Marcel was pulling him away. He said Angus must go immediately, while Georges is out of the way and before he decides to come back.

There was no time to say goodbye. Sebastien fetched the small suitcase of clothes for Angus and a cap, which he would have to wear to cover his injury. Then they were leaving, four "French" boys walking close together, talking only in whispers. I felt totally deflated and disappointed. I had imagined kissing Angus and both of us whispering that we would never forget each other, but there had been nothing.

I was just about to turn away and go back indoors, when Angus lifted his arm and waved. I waved back and blew a kiss.

Friday 21st June

I've moved back up into my bedroom. Sebastien says that they rendezvoused with Patrice last night. He had papers prepared and took Angus to meet one of the contacts who had received a message earlier, thanks to me. Poor Angus! I bet he's feeling exhausted. I don't know where he'll go from there. The network spreads a long way. Somehow they are trying to get Angus out of France, but it will be a long hard journey for him. Eventually, I hope he'll get back to Scotland. I miss him. Will I ever hear from him again? I do hope so.

Saturday 22nd June

I keep thinking about Angus. Where is he now?

Aunty Régine came round to see us. She wants to go home. Mama tried to persuade her to stay in the village for a while. She'll be safer here. But Aunty Régine won't change her mind. She wants to be at home in case there's news from Uncle Thierry.

So Papa, Sebastien and I went to Veules les Roses to see how badly her house has been damaged. As we passed along the streets, we found that many of the people of the village have returned home already. There was lots of hammering and sawing as people repaired broken roofs and replaced doors. There were a few German soldiers keeping guard on the edge of the village, but they ignored us. Other soldiers were removing burnt-out vehicles. Thankfully, there was no sign of the bodies that had littered the streets.

As we passed number 12 Rue Victor Hugo, I glanced sadly at the pile of rubble. I whispered to Sebastien that it was where Hélène lived. I had already told him about her horrible death. We climbed the steep road up to Aunty Régine's house. I was surprised to see that, apart from the door that had blown in and the panes of glass shattered on the front of the house, it didn't look too bad. Papa and Sebastien began working on the repairs. I left them to it. I needed to explore. I couldn't help the vivid flashes of memory of the battle that had raged around us. I was thinking about Angus's story.

I walked to the edge of the cliff where Yvette and I had often peered over at the sea. I found our usual spot and lay down on my front. I felt rather shaky. Only a few days ago, there were thousands of soldiers on this cliff.

I looked straight out towards the sea. I blinked and stared again. It was incredible! There, right below me, in the shallows of the low tide, sat an enormous ship. I knew it had gone aground that night, but my first close sighting of it still shook me. It's lying there, leaning slightly to one side, with several large shell holes ripped into its body. Its deck is a complete wreck of blackened and twisted metal. But, there's something even more peculiar. It's a gun, one of the large anti-aircraft guns from the deck of the ship. It's standing like an out-of-place statue in the middle of the pale sandy beach.

After a while, I looked to my left, along the beach. I could see the ruins of armoured cars, and weapons left where they had been dropped. I imagined the hundreds of soldiers still lying where they had fallen, some on the pebbles at the foot of the cliff and many others floating in the sea. The thought turned my stomach over. I've seen so many bodies in the past few days. I just wish that the killing would stop.

I turned away and closed my eyes. Suddenly, I heard a sound. I opened my eyes. A man was walking towards me along the cliff path. I stood up, embarrassed at being caught viewing the scene. He pointed at the wreck of the ship. He thought it was a terrible tragedy that such a fine ship should end like that. He told me it's called the *Cérons* and that there were hundreds of lives lost on these cliffs. I nodded, but didn't tell him that I had been so close.

Sunday 23rd June

It makes me so angry! We heard on the news last night that our Prime Minister has signed the armistice. Everyone was hoping he would be braver than that. He shouldn't have given in so easily. Adolf Hitler came to Paris to sign it. That means Germany rules France. I hate it!

Our neighbour has been along to St Valery en Caux. He says we wouldn't believe the total devastation he found there after the battle. The whole of the town centre is either flattened by shells or bombs or burnt out. I told him I had witnessed some of the fighting through binoculars from Aunty Régine's house. The fire looked so fierce, but his news shocked me, all the same. St Valery is such a nice little town. He says the best thing to do will be to demolish the lot and start again, but that won't be possible at the moment, not with the Germans having taken it over.

Monday 24th June

Aunty Régine and Charles went home this afternoon. Mama and I went with them. Aunty Régine was silent all the way. She seems to have no energy at the moment. I think it's because she hasn't heard from Uncle Thierry for a while. She's on edge, waiting for news. Grandma and Mama had tried to persuade her to stay in our village, but she refused.

Tuesday 25th June

I cycled over to Veules les Roses after school today. Aunty Régine looks better than yesterday. I think she is glad to be home. She's still very pale, but her eyes were shining. She had a letter from Uncle Thierry this morning. Mind you, she still doesn't know where he is.

But there was something else. She said she wanted to talk to me. She reminded me that I had let slip about some kind of secret work. I nodded, but I didn't know how to answer.

I still can't tell her about our secret organization. Then she mentioned the house in the Rue Victor Hugo that was demolished and the old lady that was killed. She also knows what we did for Angus. It's getting very difficult. I know I can trust her, but a promise is a promise, after all, and I gave nothing away.

In the end, I asked her what she was getting at. I was amazed at her answer. She said she can't just sit here and let the enemy tread all over us. She needs to do something. She more or less pleaded with me to help her find something to do.

I remembered what Patrice had said. We need a new contact in Veules les Roses. She would be perfect. But would she be willing to do it? I promised her I'd ask around and let her know.

Wednesday 26th June

It makes me furious. We've had news that Adolf Hitler has been sightseeing in Paris. He went to the Eiffel Tower and other famous monuments. They say he likes our capital city very much. So if this is true, why couldn't he leave it alone?

Thursday 27th June

I've asked Patrice and he's agreed to meet up with Aunty Régine. It'll be really great if she joins the network and it'll be an excuse for me to go and visit her often.

Every day, I think about Angus. I wonder if he got out of France. Perhaps he's already home. I wonder if he'll remember me.

Friday 28th June

Aunty Régine is one of us! She's our agent in Veules les Roses. I'm so excited. I cycled over to see her. Now we don't have to pretend any more and I don't have to hold my tongue when I really want to tell her everything. She's going to be needed even more, too, because Veules les Roses has become a base for German soldiers. They've taken over all the big buildings. The town hall is their headquarters with a

135

Kommandant in charge. I haven't seen him yet, but whenever I go to Veules les Roses, I see soldiers everywhere. They're too busy building concrete gun posts overlooking the sea to bother with me. Perhaps they think there'll be an invasion. I wonder if the British will come to our rescue. I hope so.

Saturday 29th June

School has finished for the summer – not that we've been able to learn much in the past few weeks, not since the 51st Highland Division arrived in our village. I somehow think Yvette and I won't be doing the same kind of summer activities as we did last year. There are too many enemy soldiers around. They often stop and search people, but so far they haven't bothered with me.

Tuesday 9th July

I just had to rush upstairs and find my diary – not in the hen house now I have my bedroom back. I have to write what

136

happened straight away. It can't wait. I'm so ecstatically happy. I met the postman outside the house a few minutes ago. He held out a letter and asked if I was Sophie Ridel. I told him I was and he gave me the letter. I studied the envelope. I thought at first it was from Anais, but the postmark was not from the area where she's living now. My heart started pounding double-time. I suddenly realized it had a Spanish stamp on it. Who do I know in Spain? Nobody – and yet…?

I dashed indoors and I ripped it open. My fingers were shaking so much I could hardly get it open. At last I pulled out a scrap of paper with a message on, written in very good French:

Dear Sophie,
I like Spain very much. The journey was long, but I am happy to be here. I will stay for a few days then I will continue my journey. Thanks to everyone, especially to you. I will never forget you.
Love AB

Angus Brown! He's safely out of France. I feel a warm glow spread right through me. He's remembered me. He says he'll never forget me. And he's sent his love! Maybe I'll see him again when the war is over. I really hope so!

Wednesday 31st July

We're busy from day to day, fighting the enemy. France has been divided into two, sort of diagonally across the middle. Marshal Pétain is in charge of the south and east, but Papa says he's a friend of the Germans anyway. That half is called Vichy France. Our half (north and west) is governed by the Germans, worse luck, so they have control of all the ports along the Channel and the Atlantic. This is why we have to keep fighting against them. They might have taken over our country, but one thing is certain. We'll never be defeated!

General de Gaulle often broadcasts from Britain. He helps raise our spirits. We remember what he said to us when he made that broadcast on the day France surrendered, that all French people should keep on fighting for our freedom. I shall always do that, right until this horrible war is over.

Historical note

In May 1940, the war in Europe started in earnest. When Hitler invaded Holland and Belgium, many thousands of British troops were sent to fight, but soon the German army fought its way into northern France and the soldiers were forced back towards the sea at Dunkerque. It seemed as if they had little chance of escape.

However, the British government put out an appeal to anyone in southern England who owned a boat to travel across the English Channel to help with the rescue of these troops. Many people responded to this appeal and a total of around 700 vessels, including hundreds of tiny craft, bigger boats and warships, came to the rescue. From 26 May to 4 June, they managed to evacuate over 338,000 soldiers from the beaches. This was codenamed Operation Dynamo.

Sadly, several thousand soldiers were killed by German firepower from the ground and from the air. Many thousands were captured and taken away to prisoner-of-war camps in Germany.

Meanwhile, thousands of soldiers of the 51st Highland Division were ordered to remain in France. They were to go to the valley of the River Somme and to defend that area under the command of the French generals.

When they arrived, they found that the French army was in disarray and that the German army was well equipped and too strong. There was much fighting, but it was obvious that the Scottish Division could not win against the might of the German command. The 51st Highlanders were then ordered to withdraw and head in the direction of Rouen and Le Havre to see if they could defend that area and keep the Germans back from the coast. The plan was that, if that failed, it might be possible for the Highlanders to embark for England from there.

However, General Rommel and the 7th German Panzer Division arrived at Rouen and Le Havre first and cut off the escape route. General Fortune, of the 51st Highland Division, chose St Valery en Caux, a small fishing port to the east of Le Havre, for the attempted embarkation.

As the Scottish soldiers approached St Valery en Caux, they were attacked by Rommel's army and the town was heavily bombarded by the German tanks and aircraft and then by the ships that were waiting off-shore to embark the soldiers. The Highlanders fought bravely. The battle raged from 10 to 12 June 1940. Some soldiers were evacuated by small boats from the port to the warships waiting off the coast, but many were killed.

The warships moved along the coast towards Veules les

Roses and the soldiers swarmed along the cliffs. Many were killed by the German tanks, machine guns and aircraft. Others were killed falling down the cliffs as they tried to escape. Many men were drowned. Around 1,300 British and 900 French soldiers managed to escape. One French warship, the *Cérons*, came in too close to the cliffs at Veules les Roses and as the tide went out, it was stuck on the sand. The men on board had to be transferred to another ship.

In the early morning of 12 June 1940, the French general surrendered to Rommel, but the Scots, not willing to give in so easily, fought on. Finally, a few hours later, General Fortune was forced to surrender under the might of the German army. Eight thousand men of the 51st Highland Division were taken prisoner and marched away to German prisoner-of-war camps. A few lucky soldiers managed to escape and, helped by the French people, returned to Britain. Those who were taken prisoner were held in the camps until they were released in 1945, five years later.

The centre of St Valery en Caux was so badly damaged that, after the war, it was totally demolished and rebuilt.

The 51st Highland Division was almost wiped out and had to be built up again with thousands more soldiers. After the Normandy landings on 6 June 1944, they were sent to liberate St Valery en Caux and the surrounding area. They arrived on 2 September 1944.

The French and Scottish soldiers who died between 9 and 12 June 1940 in that area are buried in a war cemetery on the edge of St Valery en Caux. There is also a memorial on the cliffs to the soldiers who died.

High on the east cliff above Veules les Roses is a memorial in the form of a large anti-aircraft gun from the ship, the *Cérons*. Beside the gun are three flagpoles. From the first flutters the Union Flag of Great Britain, from the second, the French *Tricolore* and from the third, the diagonal cross of St Andrew of Scotland. This memorial is directly above the wreck of the *Cérons*. When there is a very low tide, the remains of the *Cérons* can sometimes still be seen, almost 70 years on.

Timeline

1889 Adolf Hitler is born in Austria.

1919 Hitler joins the German Workers' Party.

1920 The German Workers' Party changes its name to The National Socialist Party (Nazis). Hitler chooses the symbol we know as the swastika for the party's emblem.

1921 Hitler becomes leader of the Nazi Party.

1925 Hitler publishes his book, *Mein Kampf*. Germany is going through difficult times and most of the people are poor and hungry. They begin to listen to Hitler's promises of a better life; promises he never fulfils.

1933

30 January Hitler becomes Chancellor of Germany.

26 April The Gestapo is formed and many people who disagree with Hitler are rounded up and imprisoned, tortured or killed.

1933–39 Hitler becomes more and more powerful. He builds up the strength of the German army, navy and air force.

1939

15 March Germany invades Czechoslovakia.

1 September Germany invades Poland.

3 September Britain, France, Australia and New Zealand declare war on Germany.

10 September Canada declares war on Germany.

September 1939–March 1940 is called the "Phoney War" in Britain because there is no fighting in Northern Europe. It almost seems as if there is no war.

1940

20 March Paul Reynaud becomes the new French Prime Minister.

9 April Germany invades Norway and Denmark.

10 May Germany invades Holland, Belgium and Luxembourg.

10 May The British Prime Minister, Neville Chamberlain, resigns and Winston Churchill becomes the new British Prime Minister.

13 May The German army enters France, and the British and French troops are pushed back.

15 May Holland surrenders to the Germans.

26 May The evacuation of British troops begins from Dunkerque.

28 May Belgium surrenders to the Germans.

14 June The German army enters Paris.

16 June Marshal Philippe Pétain takes over as French Prime Minister.

22 June Marshal Pétain signs an armistice with the Nazis. France is split in two. One half, to the north and west, is run by the Germans, who occupy the territory; the other half is run by Marshal Pétain, but he is working under German orders. This second area of France is called Vichy France.

16 July Hitler orders the German military to plan an invasion of Britain – Operation Sealion.

5 August The Battle of Britain begins with heavy bombing raids by German planes.

7 September The London Blitz begins.

12 October Hitler cancels Operation Sealion and turns his attention towards Russia.

1941

22 June Hitler invades Russia.

7 December Japanese planes attack the United States navy in Pearl Harbor on Hawaii in the Pacific Ocean.

8 December America declares war on Japan.

11 December Germany declares war on America.

1942 The conflict has now become a World War, with many countries joining in on both sides. There is fighting in

Europe, North Africa, Burma, Hong Kong, Singapore and other areas of the Far East.

1943

Italy, who joined in the War on the side of Germany, is invaded by the Allies.

2 February After a long time of fighting Russia, Germany at last surrenders at Stalingrad.

8 September Italy surrenders.

1944

6 June D-Day: The Allied forces invade the Normandy coast of France, to the west of the River Seine.

The Allies begin to move through France, liberating towns as they go. The German army is in retreat.

25 August Paris is liberated.

There is still much fighting in Europe and in the East. This continues well into the following year.

1945

1 May Germany announces that Hitler is dead.

7 May Germany signs an unconditional surrender.

8 May is celebrated in Europe as VE Day – Victory in Europe Day. There is still fighting in the Far East.

6 August America drops an atomic bomb on Hiroshima, Japan.

9 August America drops an atomic bomb on Nagasaki, Japan.

15 August is celebrated as VJ Day – Victory in Japan Day.

2 September Japan signs an unconditional surrender.

The war is over almost six years to the day after it began.

Picture acknowledgments

P 148 Map by Jason Cox
P 149 Imperial War Museum RML 342
P 150 Imperial War Museum RML 358
P 151 Imperial War Museum RML 368
P 152 Imperial War Museum RML 395
P 153 Imperial War Museum RML 399
P 154 Crédit photo, mairie de Veules-les-roses
P 155 © Dave Atkins, 2009

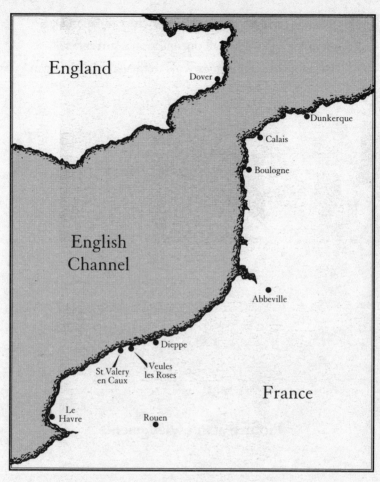

A map of northern France, from Dunkerque to Le Havre, showing the places mentioned in Sophie's diary.

General Rommel and General Fortune beside the port at St Valery en Caux after the surrender on 12 June 1940.

Burning buildings in St Valery en Caux during the battle 10–12 June 1940.

The ruins of St Valery en Caux after the battle.

12 June 1940. A Scottish prisoner of war in a kilt talking to a
German officer on the cliffs between Veules les Roses and
St Valery en Caux.

12 June 1940. French and British prisoners being marched by German guards along the cliffs from Veules les Roses towards St Valery en Caux.

The anti-aircraft gun from the *Cérons* and the three flags (British, French and Scottish) – this memorial is on the east cliff above Veules les Roses.

This Scottish memorial (a stone monolith standing in the Scottish flag) stands on the east cliff overlooking St Valery en Caux.

Experience history first-hand with My Story –
a series of vividly imagined accounts of life in the past.

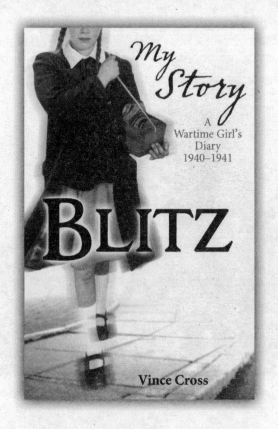

My Story

A Wartime Girl's
Diary
1940–1941

BLITZ

Vince Cross

It's 1940 and with London under fire
Edie and her little brother are evacuated
to Wales. Miles from home and missing her family,
Edie is determined to be strong,
but when life in the countryside proves tougher than in
the capital she is torn between obeying her
parents and protecting her brother...